Janice Lynn has a Masters in Nursing from Vanderbilt University, and works as a nurse practitioner in a family practice. She lives in the southern United States with her husband, their four children, their Jack Russell—appropriately named Trouble—and a lot of unnamed dust bunnies that have moved in since she started her writing career. To find out more about Janice and her writing visit janicelynn.com.

To Macy

CHAPTER ONE

FOR THE HUNDREDTH time since Riley had arrived at the engagement party Dr. Justin Brothers found himself watching her pretend she was having a good time. She wasn't.

Which didn't make sense as he knew she and Cheyenne were close friends. And Paul was a great guy. Surely Riley was happy at their engagement?

Still, if ever a woman was faking it, Riley was now. Her eyes begged to be rescued, even though she was laughing at something someone had said.

Justin wanted to don some armor and do just that.

He knew better.

Riley King fought her own battles and would cut down any man who got in her way. Or maybe it was just him she cut down.

The only place she was relaxed around Justin was in the surgery suite. There, she'd give tit for tat. He loved working with her, watching her take charge and make sure everything went smoothly. It always did with Riley at the helm.

"Go talk to her."

Justin cut his gaze to his friend Paul. "You worry about taking care of your own love-life."

Faux-punching Justin's shoulder, Paul grinned. "This whole shindig is about my love life and how awesome it is."

A pang of envy hit. Was it only last summer that Justin had almost walked down the aisle himself? That he'd thought he'd found "the one?"

How quickly things changed.

Although Justin wasn't lonely, he wasn't opposed to meeting someone special and being in Paul's shoes.

His gaze went back to Riley. The curvy nurse who was so quick to put him in his place, had captivated him from the moment he'd met her.

"You like her."

"Never said I didn't," he reminded his friend, dragging his gaze from Riley yet again. "It's more that she doesn't like *me*."

Paul gave a look of disbelief. "Never known you to strike out."

"It happens." *Unfortunately.* He couldn't recall the last time prior to Riley, but she was a biggie.

Too bad she'd laughed when he'd asked her out. Laughed and told him no in no uncertain terms.

His gaze drifted back to her, taking in the body-hugging green dress that flounced at the hem and made his eyes pop. She had her dark hair pulled up, but several tendrils had worked loose and framed her pretty heart-shaped face. At work she wore scrubs and no-nonsense shoes. Tonight she had stilettos on that made her legs look a million miles long and gave a gentle sway to her hips when she walked.

Just looking at her had Justin struggling not to reach for his collar to loosen a few buttons. Riley made him hot.

Because she was hot.

And smart, and funny, and—not interested.

Only he'd swear she was…

From across the terrace her big green eyes collided with his gaze and she failed to hide the initial flicker of awareness. The same awareness *he* felt every time they were together but that she seemed to find easy to push aside and deny.

She'd had a bad break-up a year or two ago. He didn't know the specifics, but you couldn't work in the same hospital unit and not pick up on gossip. She didn't date. Perhaps she was still hung up on her ex. That theory made the most sense but, right or wrong, the thought of her wanting another man irked him.

Cheeks blushing a rosy pink, she averted her eyes, took a drink from her champagne glass, then pretended to listen to whatever her friend was saying.

The same way Justin was pretending to listen to what Paul was saying.

Justin grimaced and told himself to stop with the Riley fascination and acknowledge the woman Paul was now introducing to him.

The single woman who'd just joined them had a hopeful look in her eyes. If she triggered half the sparks Riley did, he'd consider himself a lucky man.

Too bad he felt nothing when he looked at the tall blonde and everything when his gaze wandered back to the brunette whose gaze was on him again…

For so many reasons surgical nurse Riley King hadn't wanted to attend her coworker's engagement party. But she adored Cheyenne, and hadn't been able to think of a single excuse that wouldn't have their close-knit workgroup rallying to make sure Riley was okay.

This party was about Cheyenne—not a wake for expressing grief over Riley's jilting at the altar. She had to at least make a quick appearance, even if she knew she'd be one of the few solo attendees and would get looks of pity and offers of blind date set-ups.

No, thank you.

She didn't want pity, blind dates, real dates, or to be anywhere that had anything to do with the opposite sex and especially not with weddings.

Like this engagement party.

Still, she had to go on smiling and pretending she was having the time of her life, and that she wasn't hungry when she was actually longing to give in to the temptation of the yummy-looking calorie-laden appetizers at various locales on the beautifully decorated patio.

Even worse, she had to pretend that the engagement and wedding excitement didn't trigger flashbacks to sitting in her fancy white dress, alone on her wedding night.

Johnny's exit had just been more dramatic, but every man Riley had ever cared for had left, leaving her done with romantic involvements.

So why was her gaze constantly on the man

on the opposite side of the party venue? The very gorgeous man she couldn't keep her eyes from straying to no matter how many times she dragged them away?

Hot, steamy Dr. Justin Brothers—the heart-throb orthopedic surgeon all the females at the hospital oohed and ahhed over twenty-four-seven.

Riley didn't *ooh* or *ah* over Justin. Much. Sure, he was tall, muscular in a non-gym-rat kind of way, and had the most amazing blue eyes and smile. But she knew his type. Male—which equated to love 'em and leave 'em.

Justin was one of those fast guys who didn't waste time before declaring, "Next!" From the moment he'd arrived on the Columbia Hospital scene, he had never been with the same woman twice. He wasn't interested in pretending he'd stick around.

Wasn't that what Karen, one of his more recent exes, had told Riley when they'd bumped into each other at the grocer's? Justin was fun while it lasted, but knowing that hadn't prevented the woman from being heartbroken when he'd moved on.

Riley did not want to be the next Karen. Or Nancy. Or Stephanie.

So what if she enjoyed their hospital banter? The way he made her fight laughter more often than not? Made her fight the awareness that, although she'd sworn off romance, her body was still young and hormonal?

Regardless, she wouldn't risk a repeat of what had happened with Johnny. Not ever, ever, *ever*.

That was why she'd told Justin no when he'd asked her to dinner.

Twice.

She hadn't been sure he was serious the first time, and had figured the second time had been about wounded pride.

But if ever she was tempted to date again, Justin would be the one to make her do it.

When Justin had come to work at the hospital six months ago she had felt good old-fashioned lust surge to life. Something she'd thought impossible to feel again. Something she hadn't wanted to feel again.

Which was why she avoided him when she was outside the safety of the hospital.

The less she knew about Justin, the better.

The more she thought of him as a player—no better than any other man who'd ever walked the earth, looking for a female's heart to crush—the better.

The sooner she snuck away from this party, the better.

Why had she thought she could attend an engagement party? Wasn't that like having all her shattered dreams tossed right into her face? A vivid reminder of her own engagement party?

Romantic happiness was like a vapor. Here one moment, gone the next. Riley had sworn off pursuing that elusive mirage. Life was so much better since she had.

She gripped her glass tighter. She should have known Johnny would invade her thoughts tonight. She *had* known.

Laughing a bit too loudly at a comment someone made, Riley wanted to fall through the floor. Surely enough time had passed that she could leave without being noticed?

She glanced at her fitness watch. Her heart sank. Had she really only been there just over thirty minutes? How was that possible when it seemed hours had gone by since she'd arrived a little late, with her roommate Cassie and her on-again, off-again boyfriend Sam?

An hour. She had to stay at least an hour.

Then she could go home, change into something comfortable, eat celery while telling herself it tasted way better than chocolate, grab her six-pound Maltese terrier, and lie on the hammock in her backyard to let the night sky and her loving dog soothe away her raw nerves.

Across the room, Justin Brothers clanged his glass, causing the crowd to hush."Can I have your attention, please?"

Oh, he had Riley's attention, all right. Way too often and almost non-stop since she'd arrived and seen him putting shame to every other man present in his tailored black pants and perfect-fitting light blue button-down shirt. He'd undone a couple of buttons at his throat and rolled up his sleeves to reveal tanned mid-forearms. He looked phenomenal. Someone should put him on a billboard.

Yep, her attention was had. Which was unfortunate. You'd think an engagement party that had caused an outbreak of botched wedding memories would douse her reaction to Justin, but he still left her feeling unsettled.

"We're here tonight to celebrate Paul and Cheyenne's engagement," he continued, glancing to where the happy couple stood next to one another.

Riley's gaze followed, taking note of Paul's arm around Cheyenne's waist, his hand resting at his fiancée's lower back as she smiled up at him with her heart and a lifetime of dreams shining in her eyes.

Once upon a time Johnny had held her and she'd smiled adoringly at him, oblivious to his cheating ways.

Ugh. Riley fought a wave of nausea and finished off the champagne she wasn't supposed to drink until after the toast.

Staring into her empty glass, she grimaced. *Oops.*

Moving away from the friends she'd been talking to, she grabbed another glass from a nearby tray to participate in the toast to the happy couple.

Relationships always started with smiles and happiness. It was what came later that brought tears and heartache. Grief. Humiliation. Pity.

Drinking champagne inappropriately.

Poor Cheyenne.

Cheyenne wouldn't listen, though. Hadn't Riley already tried to warn her friend to no avail that she was making a mistake? Cheyenne had hugged her and told her that someday someone was going to come along to heal all the wounds Johnny had inflicted.

Which was naïve and completely ridiculous.

Riley did not need or want someone to come

along and "heal" her. She *was* healed—and she had learned valuable life lessons her friend had yet to experience.

Riley prayed she never would.

Tightening her hold on her new glass, she focused on where Justin was still talking, giving his toast to the couple. He was Paul's best man and he was taking his duties seriously, delivering one heck of a spiel about love and commitment.

As if he knew *anything* about those things.

"So, let's raise our glasses to Paul and Cheyenne, celebrate their love, and wish them a long, happy life together."

Riley did wish that for her friend. She just didn't believe it was possible. Still, she raised her glass, faked a smile as she clinked her glass against the nearby guests' glasses, then took a sip. A long sip that almost emptied her glass.

When she looked back toward Justin her eyes collided with his blue ones, as they often did. Probably because he was wondering why she couldn't stop looking at him.

Heaven help her, but it would be easy to fall into that man's eyes and drown in their mesmerizing depths.

She ordered her own eyes to move, to look

at the pretty landscape surrounding the porch, the ornate bushes, the small trees and colorful plants—anything other than Justin.

Her eyes refused to budge, preferring to submerge themselves in vivid blue.

Maybe he'd put a spell over her. Because not only would her eyes not avert, but her ability to fake anything vanished.

She knew it because she saw concern flicker on his face.

She didn't want his concern.

She was fine.

Better than fine.

Only…

Only nothing.

Shunning the emotions rocking her, she clamped her armor and her fake smile back into place and raised her glass to him in acknowledgement of his toast.

His gaze searching hers, he raised his glass back.

In unison, eyes locked, they took a drink.

Riley swallowed, wondering if she'd had too much as her head felt dizzy. This glass was her third and would be her last.

She rarely drank, so three glasses of champagne had to be why her insides felt so topsy-turvy. If she wasn't careful she would soon be quite tipsy. She'd only ever been drunk once—and, really, did that night even count?

Ha. That night counts for everything, the nagging voice that reared its ugly head from time to time reminded her.

That night had been the end of what she'd thought the rest of her life would be and the beginning of a very different reality.

A better reality, she reminded herself. She was strong and independent, with a job she loved, a home and dog she loved, and a good life. It was no big deal that she was faking smiles and just about everything else.

Sighing, then realizing she'd done so for real rather than just in her head, Riley jerked her gaze away from Justin, emptied her glass, and took in the partygoers around her.

Most everyone was paired up. Anywhere she went, she was one of the few singles. She'd known the engagement party wouldn't be any different. What she hadn't known was that Justin would attend alone.

On the few times she'd seen him outside the hospital he'd always had a beautiful woman on his arm.

Ugh. What good was it to not be looking at

him if she was just going to keep thinking about him? She needed to stop.

She didn't know which was worse: the flashbacks to her almost-wedding or making googly eyes at Justin. One had left her battle-scarred. The other was like stepping into the line of fire, begging to reopen wounds better left alone.

"You okay?"

Riley choked on the champagne that hadn't gone down yet. She tried to look as if the liquid wasn't clogging her airway, but quickly gave up when doing so meant not breathing. She coughed repeatedly, attempting to clear the gurgling from her throat.

"I was before you came over here and startled me," she accused, once she could form a sentence, hoping her watering eyes wouldn't ruin her mascara. "Why did you sneak up on me that way?"

Watching her closely, no doubt wondering if he needed to do some kind of medical maneuver to clear her throat, he quipped, "You mean in that walking across the terrace in plain sight way?"

She coughed one last time, took a deep breath, and appreciated it when it didn't trigger further hacking. "Yeah, that would be the way."

"For the record, my question referred to before your excellent dying from pneumonia impersonation." His lips twitched. "Glad to see you made a quick recovery."

Riley rolled her eyes. She might enjoy their banter at the hospital, but at an engagement party, with three glasses of champagne flowing through her, thinning her protective armor, not so much.

"No thanks to you," she complained, reminding herself to keep her eyes focused on his face and not let them drop to that sexy V revealed by those loosened buttons. "You could have at least slapped my back a few times."

"And have you accused me of drumming up business by cracking a few ribs?" His grin was infectious, making his eyes twinkle. "I don't think so."

Why did the man have to be so good-looking? So—so *everything*?

"I said slapping my back, not breaking bones." Although she was fighting against smiling, she gave him a stern look. "Jeez, men and their having to flex muscles every chance they get..."

He was unfazed, and his eyes danced. "You don't want to see me flex my muscles, Riley?"

Um, yeah, she'd like to see him do that...

"Not that way," she denied, gulping at her big fat lie and wondering at what she even meant. This party, maybe him, too, had her so flustered she was making no sense.

"Is there some *other* way you'd like to see my muscles flex?" He pounced on her goof. "I'd be happy to oblige."

"I'll pass, since I see all the muscle-flexing from you that I want to see in the operating room, when you're pulling and tugging on patients."

"My talents extend beyond surgery."

Heaven help her, she was about to go into a coughing fit again.

"I'm sure they do," she managed to say, knowing he was waiting.

"You should let me show you sometime."

Riley refused to take him seriously. "Ah, poor Justin. Are you upset you don't have a date tonight?"

Eyes locked with hers, he shook his head. "Quite the opposite. I purposely came alone."

Surprised, and further flustered by his answer and his look, Riley stared at him. "Why would a muscle-flexing guy like you do something like that?"

"I was hoping you'd be here without a date."

The South Carolina humidity had just gone into overdrive and was drenching her skin.

Resisting the urge to fan herself, she tilted her chin upward. "What good would that do you?"

"Based on past experience? Not one bit." Looking way too charming, he gave a self-deprecating laugh. "But a guy can hope you'll take pity and at least say yes to one dance."

Dance with Justin?

Riley gulped at the thought of wrapping her arms around his neck, of his arms around her waist. She'd need more than her hands to fan her if she agreed to that. Something along the lines of the jet blast from a Boeing 747.

"Maybe later," she answered, thinking that if she said no he'd persist, and that if she said yes he'd pull her onto the dance floor with the other couples now.

"I'm going to hold you to that."

Most likely he'd move on to one of the few other dateless women there, all of whom she'd seen talking to him at different points since arriving.

"Maybe you'd like to see the gardens? There's a small lake with a fountain just over that rise. I'm told it's worth the short walk." He gestured beyond the porch to a lighted walkway.

Getting away from the party appealed more than getting away from Justin.

She set her glass down on a table, then nodded. "Please."

Seeming surprised she'd agreed, he smiled. "You just made my night."

His smile was so genuine, so endearing, her breath caught. She fought against saying she'd changed her mind and was leaving the party she hadn't wanted to attend to begin with. Even though that was what a smart girl would do.

Her IQ was dropping by the second.

"You wish," she quipped, not waiting for him as she headed toward the path he'd pointed out.

He quickly fell into step beside her as they made their way along the cobblestoned walkway. Trimmed bushes, flowers, and solar-powered lights bordered either side, giving a sense of privacy and filling the air with the scent of sweet gardenia.

"I do, you know."

"Do what?" She didn't look at him, just carefully made her way along the path, thinking she should have gone for different shoes as four-inch heels weren't ideal for garden walkways.

When she'd chosen them she'd been thinking

of how the extra height would make her look taller, feel thinner, more in control during what she'd known would be a rough experience.

"Wish you had just made my night," he clarified.

At his response, Riley stumbled, reaching out to keep herself from falling at the same time as he moved to catch her.

She fell into his arms. Literally.

Embarrassed, she glanced up, both cursing and blessing her heels. They'd caused her to stumble, but they also gave her the vantage point to more easily look into his eyes.

Blessing? She wasn't supposed to be looking into Justin's eyes—much less easily. Nor was she supposed to be pressed against his hard body.

Oh, my!

"Well, hello, there," he teased, not stepping back from where he held her.

Neither did she. Which was a problem. Why was she not removing her body from where it was plastered to his? And why, oh, why did he feel so wonderful? So solid and chiseled to perfection?

Not to mention that his spicy clean scent was

pulling a wicked number… She'd gotten whiffs of that clean, all-man smell in the OR, but had never allowed herself to really take it in. Where was an alcohol pad when she needed one to block it out?

Unable to stop herself, Riley breathed in through her nose, filling her nostrils, her lungs, her being, with Justin.

Goodness, the man was intoxicating. His body, his smell. The way he was looking down at her.

His heart pounded hard against her chest as his gaze dropped to her mouth. She parted her lips, planning to apologize for falling, but nothing came out.

His hands trembled slightly where they pressed against her back. His throat worked as he swallowed, and then, surprising her, he closed his eyes.

The walkway lights flickered over his face, allowing Riley to see how the skin was pulled tightly across his cheeks, how he was struggling with something. Not something… With *her* and how their bodies were responding to one another.

"Justin?"

He opened his eyes.

"I feel as if I should be asking you if you're okay," she mused, still not moving out of his arms.

She'd thought it was his heart pounding against her chest. It wasn't. It was her own, banging so violently against her rib cage that he might be black and blue if he didn't step away.

He didn't. Instead, his hands moved from her lower back to caress her face.

"I'm good," he assured her.

She'd bet he was, and she wanted to know more.

Which scared her.

Terrified her.

Just as she'd worked up the strength to pry her body from his, he bent to touch his lips to hers. A soft brushing of his mouth, slow, gentle, in a show of great restraint because she felt the way his body tensed.

Lord help her for what she felt as his mouth coaxed hers to open, to allow him to explore to his heart's content.

Riley's head spun. That was how Justin made her feel. Spinning out of control.

A single moment or an eternity might have passed during their embrace. Riley couldn't have sworn one way or the other. Just knew that Justin's kiss took her beyond the realm of time, place, anything…

All that mattered was his kiss, how when she opened her eyes and looked into his what she saw weakened her knees. Mostly because what she saw there was reflected in her own for him to see.

But she didn't want him seeing behind her carefully guarded walls—didn't want anyone glimpsing behind her armor, least of all Justin.

What had she done?

She needed to run, to put as much distance between them as her high heels would let her.

But other than to tremble at the gravity of what was happening, her body didn't move.

Holding her close, he smiled. "That was worth waiting for."

Stunned at his admission, she blinked. "You were waiting to kiss me?"

Brushing a few loose hairs away from her face, he nodded. "You know I was."

No, she didn't know that.

Wrong. She *did* know.

She knew. And there was no more denying what she'd been denying for months.

What she'd been wanting for months.

Justin.

CHAPTER TWO

RILEY HADN'T INTENDED to go home with Justin.

Ha—even a few hours ago, when they'd been swirling and laughing on the dance floor, she'd still been telling herself their kiss had been a one-off.

So much for good intentions and all that jazz.

Here she was, in his bedroom, in the midst of something straight out of someone else's life, practically ripping Justin's shirt off his muscled chest.

He trailed hungry kisses over her throat, slid her spaghetti straps down her shoulders while her every nerve cell strained to be nearer to his talented lips.

She'd lost her purse somewhere. Possibly it was in the Jeep he'd driven them in to his apartment. Or maybe she'd tossed it somewhere between his front door and where they were now wrapped around each other next to his bed.

His big bed.

A big bed he'd probably brought countless women to.

Hesitation hit. Did she really want to be another notch on Justin's belt?

Abandoning their fumbling at his shirt buttons, her fingers lowered, tracing over the rich, smooth leather encircling his waist. Seriously, what was she doing? Feeling for literal notches on his belt?

She pressed her forehead to his chest, resting against the soft cotton material. Closing her eyes, she breathed in his amazing scent, full of spice and temptation.

It made women crave more.

It made *her* crave more.

Don't inhale, Riley. Do not inhale.

Wasn't that when she'd first lost her mind in the garden? When she'd allowed his scent to intoxicate her? Weaken her to his powerful sensory onslaught?

Swallowing, she clenched his belt and ordered her brain to use logic, not hormones, to calculate how she wanted to proceed.

Or not to proceed.

Unaware of her inner turmoil, he dipped his tongue into the indentation at the base of her throat as his fingers connected with her dress's zipper.

A moan rose from deep inside her chest.

She was here, in Justin's bedroom, the sole recipient of his many talents. Was she really going to tell him to stop?

He would. As wrapped up as he was in what was happening, she didn't question the fact that if she told him she'd changed her mind he'd stop.

Letting go of his belt, her hands went back to working those last few shirt buttons free. The time for stopping had gone. Just like her inhibitions, apparently.

Possibly this was happening because she'd been so emotionally raw at Cheyenne and Paul's party. And she'd drunk champagne while eating very little, because she was on yet another diet in the hopes of getting rid of the extra fifteen pounds she perpetually carried.

Or maybe she was here because what she'd seen in Justin's eyes when he'd kissed her, what she'd felt at his touch, had soothed the ever-present rawness Johnny's cruelty had dealt her.

"You taste good."

Was that why he was nibbling at her neck that way? As if her skin was nectar and he was starved?

"Sweet as honey," he continued, his lips miracle-workers at her throat.

"Too sticky," she murmured, finally freeing him of his shirt.

Wanting to look at what she'd uncovered, she attempted to take a step back. But she was too close to the bed to manage more than bumping against the king-sized monstrosity.

"Sticky sweet," he practically growled, prickling her more and more sensitized flesh with goosebumps.

His hands made their way beneath her dress, cupped her bottom, and pulled her against him.

Her entire body *tingled*. As if someone had hooked up a TENS unit and cranked the power full-blast.

Oh, wow.

He pressed against her belly, hard, tempting, promising great pleasure.

Riley wanted great pleasure.

She had heard about it, had dreamed of it a long, long time ago, but experience it? *Nada.*

Her ex sure hadn't delivered great pleasure.

Johnny had been okay in bed. Probably as good as Riley. Which should have her reconsidering what was happening now, because the last thing she wanted was Justin thinking her a dud between the sheets. She must be. Johnny wouldn't have strayed before they'd even made it down the aisle if she was any good, right?

But Justin wasn't acting as if he thought her a dud. He couldn't get enough, seemed to want to kiss her all over, touch her all over, as if he found her curves sexy rather than too fleshy. As if he found her irresistible.

Justin was *with* her, kissing her, grinding his body against hers. He was focused on her and making her feel good. He *wanted* her.

She'd regret it tomorrow. She knew she would. She knew herself too well to believe otherwise. She had to work with him, for goodness' sake.

But when his fingers hooked her panties and slid them down she couldn't lift her feet fast enough to shake free of the skimpy satin and lace material.

Not only was she doing this, but she was going to demand Justin make it worth every single recrimination she'd feel later.

With that thought, she pulled his belt free from his jeans, tossed it to the floor, then twined her fingers through the loops of his jeans and tugged him to her.

Eyes locked with his, she lifted her chin. "You only get one shot," she warned, with the bravado of a seasoned siren rather than a woman whose groom had been a no-show at their wedding. "Make it good."

Not looking the slightest bit worried about his making-it-good abilities, Justin grinned.

"I can do that," he promised, and then he did.

Slowly waking, Justin felt his lips curve when he recalled how he'd spent the night.

With Riley. Sexy, curvy Riley. With her long brown hair and big green eyes. Sweet and sassy Riley, who was all business at work, tough and forceful with her patients when they needed to be pushed, kind and gentle when they needed a soft touch, and always professional.

It was her smile that had first hooked him. When she smiled her eyes lit, dimples dug into her cheeks, and a genuine warmth exuded from her that soothed something deep inside him and yet left a raw achiness.

Last night, when he'd gone to her, he'd been thinking along the lines of chatting, going for a walk, strolling near the lake to admire the fountain, then heading back to the party to dance.

Never in his wildest dreams had Justin envisioned them heading to his apartment. To his bed.

Well, maybe in his wildest dreams. He just hadn't expected it to *happen*.

He wasn't complaining. He'd wanted her for months.

She'd been a firecracker and she had put on an impressive show. She'd met him touch for touch, kiss for kiss, demanding more until he'd given all he had to give, and then had still found the strength to give more.

He stretched his arms over his head, surprised his muscles weren't protesting his vigorous nocturnal activities. Instead he felt glorious—it was like the best runner's high.

Amazing what a night of phenomenal sex with the right woman did for a man.

And Riley was the right woman.

He'd suspected that from the moment they'd met, and finally she seemed to have quit denying there was something between them.

She hadn't said no, nor had she rolled her eyes and laughed. What she'd said had turned him inside out and shattered all doubts that they were meant to be a couple.

Anticipating the vision of Riley sleeping in his bed, her beautiful hair sprawled out on his pillow, he rolled onto his side and opened his eyes.

What?

The space where Riley should be lying was empty.

Was she already awake and hadn't awakened him?

Listening for sounds in the bathroom, or coming from the kitchen, he didn't hear the slightest creak.

With a rising sense of unease, he sat up and glanced to the bedroom floor where they'd stripped each other.

Riley's clothes were missing.

Empty bed, quiet apartment, missing clothes.

Reality gut-punched him, wreaking havoc with his earlier post-phenomenal-sex euphoria.

Riley was gone.

Why hadn't she woken him?

Getting out of bed, he grabbed a pair of shorts from a drawer, then made his way through the apartment, looking for some sign that she'd really been there and that he hadn't dreamed the entire night.

Surely she'd left a note?

A glass slipper?

Something?

Nothing.

She'd awakened, dressed, and left.

Raking his fingers through his hair, he considered his options.

He didn't have her phone number. Why hadn't he gotten it last night when he'd had the chance?

Because he hadn't expected to wake up alone. Not after the hot kisses they'd shared. The hot *everything* they'd shared.

Taking a pre-made bag of vegetables and fruit from his freezer, he dropped them into his blender, along with a scoop of protein powder, poured in some almond milk, put on the lid, then pressed the button.

Why had Riley left?

She'd enjoyed their lovemaking. She hadn't faked her responses. Not the first time or the second. She'd have told him if he wasn't pleasing her. She'd not been shy in saying what she wanted, and he hadn't hesitated in giving her that and more.

No matter. He'd thought she was through denying the sparks between them, but now she'd made how she felt clear enough. He didn't need a flashing neon sign that her being gone this morning wasn't the making of a promising relationship.

He couldn't make someone want him when

they didn't. He'd learned that almost before he'd learned to walk.

Feeling a fool, he raked his fingers through his hair, stopped the blender, then poured his smoothie into a plastic cup.

Rather than head downstairs to the condo complex's gym, he pulled out a chair at his kitchen bar and contemplated his relationship with Riley—starting from the moment they'd met. Even before then…

From the outside looking in, he and Ashley should have had it all had they married.

Only their idea of "family" had varied.

Justin had always wanted kids of his own, but planned to adopt as well. Ashley had known about the foster boys Justin was involved with, but the week before their wedding she'd told him she wouldn't be raising someone else's kids—not even his "little charity cases" whom she barely tolerated.

Justin had called off the wedding and several months later had relocated his job. He'd thought he'd focus on the boys until he met someone who wanted the same things he did—to have a big family, which included adopted and—Lord willing—birth children, and maybe a few foster kids along the way.

Then he'd met Riley.

An orthopedic nurse full of curves and sass who refused to date him but ruined his interest in every other woman.

They'd seen each other out socially a few times. But, determined not to let her get to him, as he had no desire to chase someone who claimed she wasn't interested, he'd done his best to stay away and had brought a date to each group event.

For the past few weeks he'd not even bothered dating because he hadn't been interested. And he'd known the reason.

Riley.

He'd enjoyed talking with her last night— enjoyed how, while the conversation had flowed vocally, their eyes and body had been communicating in a whole other language.

When he'd asked if she was ready to leave the party she'd not hesitated, immediately taking him up on his offer to drive her home.

Only the moment they were in his car he'd half-jokingly invited her to his place for drinks, to sit on his balcony and enjoy his view of the river.

He'd expected a flat-out no.

Instead, she'd agreed.

He should have known better. Maybe he had. But he'd been caught up in the way she'd been looking at him. And he'd barely gotten the engine turned off in the parking garage before they'd been all over each other, taking their garden kiss to another level of intensity.

Thinking back, he was surprised they'd made it to his bedroom. Had the elevator ride to his floor taken much longer they wouldn't have. The chemistry had been that powerful.

Probably because of how long he'd wanted her. How *much* he'd wanted her.

Frustrated, Justin downed the rest of his breakfast, then walked back into his bedroom so he could jump in the shower.

He'd really thought they had something special.

Too bad Riley had left.

"I wasn't expecting you to stay at Cheyenne's party after Sam and I left. How late did you stay?"

"Not too late."

Riley eyed Cassie from across the table and took a sip of her coffee. The hot liquid scalded her tongue, but she gulped the drink down rather than give any sign of unease.

"Daisy slept in my room most of the night."

"Did she?" Riley tried to make it sound as if it wasn't a big deal that her dog had stayed in Cassie's room. If Riley had been at home the dog would've been wherever *she* was. They both knew it.

"I'm not sure at what point she abandoned me," Cassie mused. "I'm guessing whatever time you came home."

Glancing down at the fluffy white dog, eyeing them in the hope they'd share some of their breakfast, Riley shrugged. "She met me at the door when I came in—" *at the crack of dawn* "—and she wanted to go outside. She crawled into bed with me after that."

"Had Sam not had to be up early for work we'd have stuck around at the party, just so I could keep an eye on you and Dr. Brothers."

Her friend waggled her brows suggestively.

"I was enjoying the fireworks exploding between the two of you."

Ugh. Could they not just go back to talking about Daisy?

Reality had hit. Although Riley had been oblivious to everyone except Justin when they'd been talking, laughing, dancing, no doubt their friends and coworkers had seen them…had taken note of the fact they'd left together.

Double *ugh*.

"Was it him who gave you a lift home?"

"No." A creepy *I-know-what-you've-been-doing* taxi driver had brought her home.

"Too bad," Cassie mused. "You seemed lost in conversation with him when you waved me off and said you'd find your own ride."

Staring into her coffee mug, Riley shrugged. "He's easy to talk to."

Easy to do a lot of things with. Things she regretted, yet wasn't sure she'd have passed up, given the choice of a redo.

"Mmm-hmm?" Cassie teased. *"Talk to."*

Knowing they were destined to have this conversation at some point, Cassie scooped Daisy into her lap, threaded her fingers into the dog's soft white fur to rub her neck, then met her friend's curious gaze.

"You two could have started an inferno with those sparks flying."

An inferno was a pretty apt description of what they *had* started. Images of the night were definitely burned into her mind.

"I drank a little more than I should have,"

Riley admitted, searching for the words to appease her friend.

Sitting her coffee mug on the table, Cassie leaned forward. "You left with him, didn't you?"

Riley grimaced. "Do we have to have this conversation before I've finished my first cup of coffee?"

Cassie clasped her hands together and made a gleeful noise. "Which means you did!"

Riley's face instantly heated. Cassie was her best friend, knew all the details of her wedding gone awry. She understood when Riley said she wasn't interested in going back down that road.

"We all make mistakes," she admitted, thinking hers were typically super-sized.

"No!" Cassie gasped, her bottom lip going into a disappointed pout. "Dr. Brothers wasn't any good?"

"He was—*phenomenal*—good." She couldn't bring herself to say otherwise. "Just..." she stroked Daisy's fur "...I shouldn't have had sex with a coworker."

"There's no hospital rule about dating coworkers." Cassie dismissed her comment with a wave of her hand. "I'd know, since I'm dating a really hot emergency room nurse."

There *was* that.

"Justin and I aren't dating," Riley pointed out, staring at Daisy as if she was trying to convince the dog. "Last night was a one-off fluke. Nice, but no big deal."

"*Nice?* The man is gorgeous enough to make even me look twice, and I'm gaga over Sam." Cassie shook her head. "I can't believe you're describing sex with Dr. Brothers as 'nice!' Guess he'd be too good to be true if he was the total package."

Justin *was* the total package. Witty, kind, attentive, gorgeous…*hot in bed*.

Stop thinking of him that way, she scolded herself, her temples pounding.

Still, letting Cassie think poorly of Justin didn't sit well.

"Last night was better than nice—way better. But it doesn't matter. What happened was one night. Nothing more."

Her friend sipped her coffee, obviously processing what Riley had said.

"I can't say this doesn't surprise me, because it does," Cassie began. "I thought— Oh, never mind what I thought. If that's all he wants it's his loss. You're a great catch."

Even her best friend assumed it must be Justin who didn't want to continue their relationship. Because no one in their right mind would assume a slightly chubby plain Jane wouldn't jump at the chance to be with him anytime he crooked his talented finger.

They were probably right. But she wasn't giving Justin the opportunity to be the one to say, *Thanks, but no thanks.*

She liked her life just as it was. She'd worked hard to get Johnny's voice out of her head, and on most things had succeeded.

She liked not having to worry about making anyone happy but herself. Not having to walk on eggshells because of her many flaws, or worry about starting over if the person she'd built her world around found someone new and left her.

Riley reached for the small golden cross she wore at her neck and toyed with when she was nervous or agitated.

It wasn't there.

Her stomach knotted.

It had to be.

She touched her neck again, feeling around on her throat. Panic gurgled from her belly upward. No! She hadn't lost—

Riley's airway tightened.

Her necklace was gone.

Sitting Daisy down, she stood, patted her

neck, shook out her clothes, looked around on the floor.

Nothing.

Panic rose, clogging her throat.

"What's wrong?" Cassie asked.

"My necklace." Riley fought back tears, tracing back in her mind when she last recalled having it.

"The one your mother gave you?"

Riley nodded, feeling bereft, as if she'd lost a part of her mother. Had she had it on the night before at the party? She couldn't remember—couldn't recall if she'd put it on after changing out of her scrubs at the hospital. Was it possible she'd lost it there?

She'd check at the hospital, call Cheyenne, see if anyone had found the necklace at either place. She hoped so. She'd hate never to wear the precious gift again. It had been the last thing her mother had given to her.

Or she might have lost it was while she was with Justin. Had she still had it on in his Jeep? At his condo?

In his bed?

Justin scrubbed for surgery. He had two hip replacements on his schedule today. One on a fifty-two-year-old male with severe arthritic changes, and another on a thirty-year-old who'd had high-dose steroids administered repetitively in primary care that had resulted in necrosis of the hip joint. Both were total replacements, and would be mentally and physically demanding.

And emotionally. Because both meant being in the operating room with the woman he'd thought about almost non-stop since she'd left him.

Riley frustrated him. He kept telling himself to forget her. Then he'd remind himself that he'd been telling himself that for months and it hadn't worked. Had he really thought it would after Saturday night? After their sweet garden kiss and how much fun they'd had at the party? How much fun they'd had *after* the party?

Even the boys had commented that he wasn't his usual upbeat self during their fishing trip yesterday afternoon.

It hadn't been a fish he'd wanted to catch, but a woman he'd thought he'd hooked, but who'd gotten away.

He'd already gotten involved with one woman who hadn't wanted the same things as he did. Obviously Riley didn't either or she wouldn't have left.

He seriously needed to move on.

Maybe telling himself that would work this time.

Knowing he'd way over-scrubbed, Justin made his way into the operating room where he'd spend the next few hours.

Good thing Bernie Jones' hip would require all his attention.

Riley had been dreading this moment since she'd left Justin's. The moment they came face-to-face.

Well, not face-to-face, since they both wore surgical masks and were covered from head-to-toe.

Still, their eyes were visible beneath their protective shields.

Justin's eyes were expressive.

Usually.

Exactly as it should be—even if it did sting a little—he'd not bothered to look her way yet. He'd just entered the operating room and asked to start the check-in procedure.

What had she expected? For him to say something directly to her?

Hello, Riley, so how about Saturday night?

She didn't want him to do that—would have

been mortified if he had. So why the disappointment that he was ignoring her?

Maybe it was lack of sleep making her crazy. Certainly, despite knowing she'd made the right decision, she'd struggled to keep her mind off Justin.

And off her missing necklace.

Yeah, that was why, when she finally had slept, it had been after tears shed over her lost treasure and nothing to do with Justin.

She needed to ask him if he'd found her necklace. No one had found it at Cheyenne's party or anywhere else. When she could get him alone, she'd ask.

Not that she wanted to be alone with him, but she couldn't very well ask if he'd found her necklace at his condo without raising a few eyebrows. They'd already caused enough eyebrow-raising on Saturday night.

She was working as the nurse overseer that day. Her job was to make sure everyone had what they needed, that a sterile field was maintained, and that everything went the way it should and was recorded accurately.

An anesthesiologist, his assistant, a scrub tech, a circulator, and a scrub nurse were also in the room, along with their patient.

"Bernie Jones, age fifty-two. Controlled hypertension and no other known health conditions," Riley informed the, starting the check-in while double-checking the patient's ID bracelet. "No known drug allergies."

"I will be performing a minimally invasive left hip arthroplasty," Justin began, and then proceeded to give a one-minute synopsis of what the planned surgery entailed. Sometimes that changed, as unexpected issues arose, but for the most part the hip replacements performed at this hospital were uneventful.

The man was an excellent surgeon. The best she'd ever worked with. Many of the other orthopedic surgeons, although talented, were moody, sometimes socially awkward. Not Justin. Everyone on the unit loved working with him.

Always upbeat, he usually chatted while performing whatever procedure they had going. Thus far today, however, he'd been all business.

Which was fine. Only…

Oh, no—no onlys.

Justin needed his full focus on his job and so did she.

The scrub nurse had the patient properly positioned. The anesthesiologist had the patient completely unaware of what was happening to and around him. And, with the patient lying flat on his back, Justin made an eight-centimeter incision. Once he had the incision made, he placed soft tissue retractors in front of and behind the femoral neck, exposing the hip joint.

"Scalpel."

The surgical tech handed Justin the cutting tool, which he took and released the capsule to expose the femoral head and the acetabulum. He studied the area a moment, made another tiny cut. When he was happy with what he'd done he used a protractor to work on the unhealthy acetabulum, removing bone spurs and diseased tissue.

Reminding herself that she was responsible for what every person in the room was doing, not just Justin, Riley pried her gaze away from his skilled hands and took in each member of the OR team. Anesthesia was closely monitoring vitals, and everyone else was attentively doing what they should be.

Her gaze went back to where Justin worked. He'd dislocated the hip and was inserting a large screw into the acetabulum. Once the screw was securely embedded in the bone he exposed the femoral head more fully and finished removing the capsule.

While the anesthesiologist chatted with his assistant about a recent sailing trip he had made, Justin painstakingly removed the femoral head with an oscillating saw, cleaned the acetabulum, then went about rebuilding the joint with prosthetics.

All in all, the surgery took just over two hours to complete.

When he was finished, Justin's gaze lifted and sought Riley's.

What she saw there had her stomach churning more than any bone-cutting surgical procedure she'd ever witnessed.

His eyes glittered with what she could only label as *hurt* because she'd pushed him away—although more likely that was just his wounded pride she was seeing. But there was also curiosity as to why she'd done so. And something more that she could only think of as warmth—not that that made any sense.

None of what she saw made sense except the curiosity. He probably wasn't used to women walking away from him, so no doubt that did have him puzzled.

Leaving him had been her being proactive on

preventing heartbreak. A pre-emptive strike. She'd left before he had.

Maybe if Justin hadn't been quite so handsome, had been something more ordinary than an orthopedic surgeon, not quite so fabulous, she might have risked a relationship. Doubtful after what Johnny had done, but maybe.

Someone so good-looking, so successful, was destined to break her heart if she gave him the chance.

"Good job," he praised the team, still holding her gaze.

Something flashed in the blue depths that suggested he saw more than she wanted him to see, that he knew she warred within. She wanted to look away, to mask her eyes from his. With each passing second her heart pounded harder.

Just as it reached the point of thundering in her ears, he broke contact and headed out of the operating suite.

"Wonder what was up with Dr. Brothers. He was quieter than usual," the recorder said as soon as Justin was out of the room.

Riley stared down at the surgical tray.

"But he's still a pleasure to work with. If only all orthopedic surgeons were as easy to be with in surgery as that man," the assistant observed.

"If only all orthopedic surgeons were as easy on the eye as that man," the surgical tech teased with a waggle of her brows.

Riley said nothing and prayed that Sheila, the scrub nurse, wouldn't say anything either. Sheila and her husband had been at Cheyenne's party.

"Looked like you were all cozy with him on Friday night, Riley," said, Sheila giving her a knowing look. "I saw you leave together."

Ugh. Of course Sheila had seen. And now she'd mentioned that. In front of the whole team.

"Really? Lucky you…" The surgical tech sighed.

Rather than answer Sheila, or acknowledge the surgical tech, who looked amazed that Justin had been with her, Riley shrugged and went about preparing the patient to be rolled to the recovery room.

What could she say?

Why, yes, that was me, all cozied up with Justin. And guess what? The man is pure genius between the sheets!

Yeah, that wasn't happening.

Nor would she tell them that she'd left before he'd awakened and had the opportunity to tell her to leave.

Sheila was right, though. Justin had been

particularly subdued. Normally he would have made chitchat, and most definitely would have said something directly to her. He'd have made small talk, teased her about Daisy and how she needed to get a real dog, or he would have lingered after surgery to chat for a few minutes.

He'd done none of those things.

As much as she hated to admit it, the fact that their Saturday night escapade had created this rift in their work relationship, leaving things awkward, stung.

Justin was used to one-night stands, so what had happened shouldn't be a big deal. But the others were right. He hadn't behaved normally. He'd been as tense as she had.

Was it because she'd been the one to leave? Or could she have misjudged how casually he saw sex and Saturday night hadn't been quite as run-of-the mill for him as she'd thought?

CHAPTER THREE

IT HAD BEEN a long day, but Riley had made it through her first day at work after "that night," as she'd dubbed Saturday.

She wasn't sure what she'd expected, but she shouldn't have worried. Except for that lingering look after he'd finished the surgery Justin had ignored her. That would hopefully put to rest the rumors flying around that they were an item after being seen together at Cheyenne's party.

More than one person had questioned her about her relationship with Justin. The fact that people actually believed they might be an item floored Riley. Couldn't they see she was nothing like the women he dated? She wasn't tall, thin, bordering on perfect.

She'd be a sitting duck, just asking to be dumped again, if she got involved with Justin.

Grabbing her bag from the locker, she headed out of the nurses' changing area and down the long hallway toward the elevator bank.

Just as she got into an open car Justin stepped inside—then realized who she was, and paused midway to pressing his floor number. His jaw tightened, and for a moment she thought he was going to either wait for the next elevator or take the stairs.

Riley bit into her lower lip, telling herself to let him leave, but then heard herself saying, "It would be silly for you to get out."

He faced her. "You're sure?"

She nodded.

The elevator was empty other than the two of them, and it was with reluctance that Riley watched the door close behind Justin.

"You did a great job on the hip replacements today," she rushed out, feeling the need to fill the silence.

"Seriously? One minute you're sneaking out of my condo and the next you want to make small talk?"

"Fine…" she breathed, knowing she deserved his question. But how could she explain that she'd missed their usual camaraderie when she'd been the one to leave? "I won't say another word and we'll ride the elevator in complete awkward silence."

Her insides trembled. So did her lower lip. She

felt Justin's shoulders sag more than saw them as she refused to look up.

"I'm sorry."

She didn't respond, just willed herself to be strong. But how could she hold tough when just being near him was setting her nerve-endings on edge? Setting her memories ablaze? When the taste of him lingered on her lips and in her mind? When she craved his mouth against hers?

Ugh.

She would not put herself through this. She just wouldn't.

"Hell, Riley…" He sounded as upset as she felt. "This isn't easy for me, you know."

That had her gaze lifting. "You think it's easy for *me*?"

His eyes searched hers. "Isn't it?"

Was that what he thought? She must be a better actress than she'd given herself credit for.

"People were talking about us today. I didn't like it." She hesitated, and then, glancing away, admitted, "More than that, I didn't like it that you didn't talk to me."

"I didn't know what to say."

"You normally have no trouble talking to me," she reminded him.

"I normally haven't had sex with you, then woken up in bed alone."

"There is that." Riley leaned back against the elevator wall, looked up—and lost her breath as her gaze locked with his emotion-filled one.

He really did seem to be struggling with this as much as she was. He looked as torn and confused about what had happened as she was, and wondering where they went from here.

She sank her teeth into her lower lip as she considered him—as she considered her own conflicted thoughts and emotions.

She'd looked into those eyes when they were filled with passion, had laughed with him, smiled at him, felt so at ease with him Saturday night.

His seeing her naked could have been so awkward—could have triggered so many negative memories of Johnny's harsh comments about her size and many other failings. Instead Justin had made her feel beautiful, sexy, confident. Not once had he looked at her or responded to her with anything other than complete and utter fascination.

And Justin being fascinated with her—her body, her words, her desires—had been heady. Addictive. Making her want more. Lots more.

She still wanted more. As evidenced by the heat building inside her at being near him, alone, in an elevator, and knowing what he was capable of.

She gulped.

As if he had read where her mind had gone his gaze dropped to her lips and his eyes darkened. "Riley, I really am sorry. I—"

The elevator came to a stop and the door slid open. Two suited men boarded, nodded toward them, then went back to their conversation.

Justin didn't resume speaking—for which Riley was grateful. She didn't want the suits privy to their conversation. But she wanted to know what he'd been about to say.

When they got off the elevator they headed in silence toward the employee parking area. She bit her already sore lower lip as they walked near to one another and yet so far away.

She should have known this would happen. This horrible awkwardness.

She *had* known.

Justin had never been one for dancing around an issue, and he truly didn't understand why Riley hadn't woken him.

He'd had to bite his tongue in the elevator. He

wanted to talk to her—needed to talk to her to understand what had happened between them. But he knew Riley wouldn't appreciate their having a serious conversation in front of others.

Once they got outside the building they'd headed for the employee parking lot. Although only a few feet apart physically as they walked together toward their cars, miles separated them in every other way.

He couldn't hold back any longer. "Why did you leave?"

"There was no reason to stay."

Ouch. Did she truly believe that? "I can think of a few."

She sighed. "Don't look a gift horse in the mouth, Justin."

Confused, he stopped walking. "Not sure I follow."

"My leaving made things simpler for both of us."

"By…"

"By letting us not have to pretend what happened meant anything."

Having to remind himself that they were in the hospital's parking lot, Justin contemplated what Riley said. "Who says it didn't mean anything?" he asked.

Her gaze cut to his. She looked stunned for such a brief moment that he thought he might have imagined the flash of vulnerability.

"Good sex counts for something, eh?" she said.

His faltering ego surged a little. "You admit the sex was good?"

Her cheeks went bright pink. "Would you believe me if I denied it?"

"No." He knew better. "Which is why I was shocked to find you'd left. We could have spent the day together."

She shifted her weight, looking more and more uncomfortable with their conversation. No wonder. They were still standing in the employee parking lot.

"This isn't the best place to have this conversation," he admitted. "Maybe we could grab a bite to eat?"

Obviously shocked at his suggestion, she met his gaze and appeared ready to tell him no. It wouldn't be the first time.

"No strings attached," he added. "Come and talk with me so we can get past this weirdness between us. It seems neither of us likes it."

"I—I have to let Daisy out. Sorry."

He started to point out that they could meet

up afterward, but she'd already taken off toward her car.

Well, that hadn't gone the way he'd hoped.

Then again, what had he expected? She'd left his bed without waking him.

Riley tapped her fingers against the steering wheel as she drove toward the park. She'd have plenty of time to hit the trail before sunset. She had to get out of the house and burn some of her nervous energy. And she needed to run as she hadn't exercised over the weekend.

Sex with Justin had burned more than few calories, though.

Ugh.

"I have to stop thinking about him," she said out loud, hoping that would make it happen.

Not true. She *needed* to think about him and figure out what his odd behavior in the OR meant. What his asking her to dinner meant. Even more, she needed to figure out why it mattered so much.

Shouldn't she just let it go? Not worry that their working relationship felt changed forever and just be grateful she'd escaped unscathed otherwise?

Only she didn't feel grateful. She felt bereft of his friendship.

So why had she refused dinner?

She gripped the steering wheel tighter. He'd said no strings attached when she'd hesitated. Why hadn't she gone?

For the same reason that for so long she'd only interacted with him at the hospital.

Justin was dangerous to her peace of mind.

To her peace of heart.

Seeing him in the elevator had flustered her, so that she hadn't even thought to ask about her necklace. She'd ugly-cried at the loss, so how could she have not remembered to ask? Then again, if he'd found it, he'd have told her, surely?

She pulled into an empty parking space, happy to have found one so quickly as the lot was almost full.

Daisy whimpered from the back seat, where she was inside her carrier.

"I know, girl. Give me a minute and I'll have you out of there," she promised, opening the door, then Daisy's crate. She snapped a leash to Daisy's collar. "We're going to work off some steam, aren't we?" she cooed as she put the car key fob inside the zipped pouch at her waist.

Car locked. Dog on leash. She ticked the items off in her head before turning toward the trail.

Were her eyes playing tricks on her?

Not twenty feet away Justin was stretching.

She'd not told him where she was headed. Had she subconsciously chosen this park because she'd gotten glimpses of him running there in the past? If so, was she crazy? Why would she *do* that?

He hadn't seen her yet. She could leave without him knowing she'd been there.

Instead, she took a deep breath and went to face what seemed inevitable.

Because she needed to ask him about her necklace—not because she'd latch onto any excuse to talk to him.

Justin stretched his hamstrings, then straightened, planning to take off down the trail.

Instead, he almost fell over.

"Riley!" he exclaimed when she jogged over to him. She must have parked on the far side of the lot. Then his gaze dropped. "Who do you have here?"

At his question, the living white mop that was wearing pink bows just above its ears barked.

Looking uncomfortable, Riley squatted down

to pet the Maltese terrier with its big dark eyes. "Meet the infamous Daisy. She's here to protect me."

Wishing he knew how to make the awkwardness between them go away, he decided to keep it light, so he arched a brow at the dog that couldn't weigh more than six or seven pounds. "What's she going to do? Yap someone into submission?"

Still rubbing the dog's neck, with a slight smile Riley warned him, "Don't underestimate the annoyance factor of a small dog's bark. From experience, I assure you there are times you'll do most anything to quieten it."

"You run with her?"

"She's home alone all day while I'm at work. I'm not leaving her there again while I run."

Justin was impressed by her thoughtfulness. Was even more impressed that she'd come over to him and was carrying on a semi-normal conversation.

He eyed the dog, who had stopped barking and was now sniffing his running shoes. "She runs?"

"Sometimes." Riley laughed. "She's quite the princess, but I adore her."

Her confession eased the tension that he'd

been carrying from the moment he'd realized she'd bailed on him and that had multiplied tenfold after their conversation at the hospital. He still needed to unwind, though. And nothing did that the way running did.

"But no worries," she assured him, her pretty green eyes sparkling. "If we can't keep up with those long legs of yours we'll just lag behind."

She planned to run with him?

Earlier she'd told him not to look a gift horse in the mouth. At that time he hadn't agreed. Currently he was going to take her advice and go with it.

"For that matter," she continued, "Daisy gives me the perfect excuse if I fall behind."

He'd walk if that was what it took to spend time with her. They needed this. At least he did. From the moment he'd awakened to find her gone he'd been trying to figure out where he'd gone wrong.

"How many days a week do you run?" she asked as they fell into step beside each other, Daisy trotting along beside them.

Moving more slowly than he normally would, he shrugged. "Depends on my surgery schedule. Every day, if I can. I enjoy running. It keeps me sane. How about you?"

"I don't run because I *enjoy* it."

He glanced toward her. "Then why?"

"It's part of my weight-loss plan."

Her weight-loss plan? "I've seen you naked. You don't need to lose weight." Realizing what he'd said, worrying she would shut him out, he grimaced. "Sorry."

Jogging, Riley remained silent.

Wanting to move past what he'd said, he asked, "What kind of weight-loss plan are you on, Riley?"

"Low-calorie, low-fat, low-carb, regular exercise, water only—and weekly séances and exorcisms to rid me of the starving little demons inside me who love to eat. You name it, I'm trying it."

Thankful that she'd not clammed up, Justin felt his lips twitch at her reply. "How's that working out?"

"Not as well as I'd like—obviously. And I find no humor in it. Not everyone can look as good as you, Mr. Washboard Abs. Some of us have to torture ourselves just to maintain a semi-healthy weight."

"Thanks." Trying not to puff out his chest at her compliment, he grinned. "For the record, I think you look amazing."

She rolled her eyes. "Flattery will get you no-where. I have eyes, a mirror, and thighs that are more flab than fab. But I'm working on that." She let out a sigh. "Thus the torture."

He gave her a skeptical look. "What exactly is it you're hoping to accomplish with all this torture?"

"To drop fifteen pounds."

From his vantage point beside her he let his gaze travel down her body, then shook his head. "You don't need to do that. You look great just as you are."

"Yeah, if you like chunky."

Did she really believe that? Despite her light tone, he realized that she did. She was always so confident at the hospital, and had seemed so in charge on Saturday night, that to hear the very real vulnerability shocked him.

"I don't know why you're under the impression you're chunky. Take it from me—your curves are sexy as hell."

"I…um…thank you."

She didn't say any more, just ran in silence, but he could tell his compliment had both pleased and disconcerted her. Was it her ex who'd put the crazy notion that she was over-weight in her head?

Justin wished she could see herself through his eyes—then she'd know how beautiful she was.

"Daisy does like jogging, doesn't she?"

Having teased her about the dog for months, he deemed that the safest topic. Not that he necessarily wanted safe conversation, but he'd tried being direct earlier and that had gotten him nowhere.

"I told you," she reminded him, smiling as her gaze dropped to where the dog was happily keeping up. "She's a good girl—aren't you?" She baby talked to the dog. "Of course she prefers riding to exercising, and I'll be having to carry her before we're done. Takes after her mama, don't you?"

Justin laughed. Riley obviously loved her dog. She talked about her at work often enough. He'd teased her into telling him about Daisy's adventures numerous times since learning of her pet. Seeing her with the dog now, introduced another side of Riley.

"How long have you had Daisy?"

"I adopted her from a local shelter after… last year. I went to the shelter planning to get a guard dog." She gave a self-derisive laugh. "I left with this sweetheart instead."

"So when I tease you and say that you should have gotten a bigger dog I'm not far off the mark?"

"I've no regrets over my choice."

Too bad she couldn't, or wouldn't, say the same about Saturday night.

"What about you?" she asked. "Do you have a dog? Or are you more a cat kind of guy?"

He shook his head. "No pets—which you know. You've been to my place."

There he went, reminding her of Saturday night again. If he really wanted to keep the tension down he was going to have to do better.

"True. I…" She winced. "Sorry. I wasn't thinking."

"No problem. Maybe I should get one, though—so I can train it to wake me up when beautiful women sneak out of my bed."

What was *wrong* with him? He wasn't supposed to be poking the subject with a stick.

"You foresee women sneaking out of your bed as a recurring event?"

"I didn't foresee it being an event *ever*," he admitted, hoping she wouldn't freeze. "I'd like to think any woman I'd invited into my bed wouldn't want to sneak out."

She gave a little shrug. "I woke up and thought leaving was the best thing for both of us."

"You were wrong. At least from my perspective."

She jogged beside him in silence for a few minutes. Then, "What would be different had I stayed there?"

Her question caught him off-guard. More the fact that she'd asked than the fact that he hadn't considered it. He had.

"I'd like to think you'd have given our coworkers a different response to their asking about us today."

She kept her gaze focused on the path ahead of them. "What kind of different response?"

Did she really not know? Or did she just want to hear him say the words out loud?

"I've not kept it a secret that I want to date you, Riley."

She turned toward him, stumbled a bit, causing him to reach out to steady her. She shook his hand away, then resumed her previous slow but steady pace.

"I didn't take you seriously."

"Way to deflate a guy's ego…" he half-teased.

"That's not what I meant. I—I meant the

opposite, really. I'm surprised you want to date me."

Once again the vulnerability in her voice surprised him. It was what he'd seen glimmering in the depths of her eyes so brightly at Cheyenne and Paul's party—what had lured him to her despite his determination to stay away since she'd shot down his dinner offers.

"Why would that surprise you? You're smart, funny, beautiful…we enjoy talking with one another." *Enjoy so much more with one another.* "We have great chemistry. Why wouldn't I want to date you?"

She hesitated long enough to reinforce the fact that his response truly had caught her off-guard.

"I'm not like the women you usually date," she said finally.

He didn't see the connection between that and her saying no. That she wasn't like other women he'd dated was a huge plus in his eyes.

"I haven't dated anyone in a couple of months," he pointed out, "and the reason I want to date you is that you're different."

Her intake of breath was her answer. She hadn't considered that her being different was a *good* thing. How could she not see how crazy he was about her?

"You are different, Riley," he assured her. "In a great way. That's why I want to spend time with you."

Giving a warning to Daisy, she came to a halt, put her hands on her hips and regarded him. "Let's be real," she said a bit breathily. "Most women are different from the real-life Barbie dolls you date."

Jogging in place, he looked back at her. "I haven't dated a woman solely based upon her looks since I was a teenager." Had he even then? "Any woman I've dated has had more going for her than just looks."

But even if looks were a qualifier Riley had nothing to worry about. Everything about her appearance appealed to him. Her eyes sparked with a green fire that would dull any gem. A soft sheen of sweat glistened over her skin, giving it a healthy glow. And her body… Well, he knew how her curves fit perfectly against him.

Still, he wanted her to understand about Saturday night—that he hadn't meant things to proceed as fast as they had, that she was more to him than a one-night stand. How did a man go about saying that to a woman who seemed not to want any more than that without coming across all wrong?

"Such as?" she asked, and then, having obviously caught her breath, took off down the trail again, Daisy quickly taking a slight lead.

"The last woman I dated was a veterinarian who volunteers with a local Spay Your Pet program," he pointed out as he fell into step beside her, not wanting her to think he was a total loser.

But he didn't really want to discuss his exes. At some point he'd explain about Ashley, but he got the impression Riley would add his failed relationship with her to what she perceived as his revolving dating door.

"If I'd had a dog," he continued, "she'd have been handy to have around."

"You *don't* have a dog, though, so that couldn't have been your reasoning."

He might almost believe that was jealousy tingeing Riley's reply.

"Stacey was a nice woman," he defended. She had been. She'd also been in love with someone else. "My mother still volunteers at her Spay Your Pet program a couple of times a month."

"Does your family live close, then?"

"My parents live just south of Columbia. The rest of our wild bunch are scattered within a thirty-mile radius. We get together every week or two for dinner."

"You've always lived here, then?"

He nodded. He'd been lucky when he'd been placed with the Brothers family at such a young age and they'd adopted him. So many kids never got any family—much less one like he'd had.

"My family is close." In more ways than one. "I've no desire to move away. What about you?"

She hesitated a few seconds before answering. "I moved to Columbia for university, but I grew up in a small town close to the Florida state line."

"You never thought of going back after graduation?"

She shook her head.

"I'm glad you stayed. Otherwise we wouldn't have met."

She rolled her eyes. "You *sure* you're used to running? You may be suffering from lack of oxygen."

"Because I'm glad we met?"

She stared straight ahead, but rather than answer came to another stop.

"Need a break?"

She shook her head. "Nope. Going to give Daisy a drink. I should have when we stopped a few minutes ago. You go ahead—don't let us hold you up."

"I'm in no rush."

He knew better. If he took off he wouldn't see her again until they were back at their vehicles. If then. He wouldn't put it past her to find a way to leave without his knowing again…

CHAPTER FOUR

DAISY HAD BEEN as good an excuse as any to put a halt to their conversation. Riley recognized her action for what it was.

She couldn't figure Justin out. If she took him at face value he seemed too good to be true. And things that were too good to be true were exactly that. Not true.

Unzipping her pouch, Riley took out a small container of water and let Daisy lap from the lid. When she was done drinking the dog sat down and stared up at Riley with big eyes.

"Had enough, girl? I don't blame you. If I looked as good as you I'd demand to be carried too," she cooed, earning a few hand-licks as she picked her up and cuddled her in her arms.

"All you have to do is say the word?"

Riley blinked at Justin. "Pardon?"

"I'll carry you anywhere you want to go," he offered, his eyes full of challenge.

"You'll *carry* me?"

Grin on his face, he nodded.

"That would be humorous. Not that I'd do it to you," she added quickly, patting her thighs. "Wouldn't want to hurt the hospital's best orthopedic surgeon's back."

His smile fading a little, he met her gaze. "Don't do that."

"What?" she asked, not following what he meant.

"Insult yourself or imply that you aren't perfect."

Heat flooded her face, but she stood her ground as she stroked Daisy's fur. "Stating facts isn't insulting oneself and no one is perfect— least of all me."

"Then you were insulting *me* when you implied I'd hurt my back if I carried you?"

"I— Can we just get back to jogging?"

He studied her a moment, then challenged, "Hop on, Riley."

"What?"

"You heard me. I need to prove that carrying you is no big deal. My man card demands it."

She looked toward the evening sky and shook her head. "You're crazy."

"Think of it as part of my workout," he teased,

leaning forward a little and lowering himself for her to hop on.

She rolled her eyes. "I should—just to teach you a lesson."

His eyes sparkled. "I'm always up for learning a new trick."

Something in the way his eyes glittered, as if he didn't think she'd do it, had her contemplating taking his challenge. Made her want to. How rebelliously teenagerish of her.

"Scared I'll drop you?" he pushed.

"No, that didn't cross my mind." It hadn't. "I just don't think Daisy would like me riding on your back."

"Think she'd be jealous? You could hold her."

His grin was full of mischief—as if he could read her thoughts and knew she was tempted, as if he wanted to tempt her further.

"I'm all sweaty," she warned him, not believing she was even considering taking up his offer.

"It's summertime in South Carolina. Everyone is sweaty. Come on, Riley. Have some fun."

A vision of Johnny telling her to do the same, to "have some fun," echoed through her head. What was it he'd said? That she lacked spontaneity and he was glad he'd realized before it was too late?

She'd been grieving her mother's death. Of *course* she'd been "uptight" and "dull."

That didn't mean she was now.

She narrowed her gaze at this grinning hunk, pushing her outside her comfort zone.

"If you drop me," she warned, "'fun' isn't the word I'm going to use."

His eyes glittered. "If I drop you, you can use any word you like. Ready?"

It was probably because of Johnny's taunts that the silliness of riding piggyback with Justin through the park, even if only for a few yards, tempted her so much. Maybe Johnny had been right. How long had it been since she'd done something carefree and out-of-character?

When had she become boring?

She was content with her life, or maybe she'd just been treading water. But something about Justin made her entertain things she wouldn't otherwise consider.

That's not necessarily a bad thing, that nagging inner voice assured her.

Justin bent lower, so she could grab hold of him around his neck. "Your chariot awaits, ma'am."

She shoved aside the last bit of doubt and instantly felt lighter.

"Hang on," she told him, putting Daisy back on the ground. "I have to make sure we don't tangle up her leash."

"Can't have that."

"Now we're ready." She wrapped her arms around Justin's neck and hopped a little, to make it easier for him to scoop her legs around his waist. Once he had her up Daisy gave a yap, clearly not liking that Riley was on his back.

"Shh, Daisy—stop that."

But Daisy kept barking and Riley kept shushing.

"This may not work," Riley warned Justin when the dog didn't calm. "She's small, but she can make a person wish he was deaf."

"She won't bite?"

"She never has before."

"Then hang on."

With Daisy still yapping at his feet, Justin took off in a playful trot.

They wouldn't win any speed contests, but they weren't trying to go full force—more just having fun. Being with Justin *was* fun. It was also a bit nerve-racking to have her legs wrapped around his waist, her arms wrapped around his neck, for his skin to be against hers, to feel his body heat, his strength against her...

She *so* shouldn't be thinking the things she was thinking.

Daisy gave a few more yaps, but then settled, just looking up at them as she kept pace.

Justin made carrying her seem like nothing. But having her body wrapped around his, even in this innocent way, wasn't nothing—not when he made her feel *everything*. When their skin-to-skin contact, even though innocent, felt nothing of the sort.

Her thighs tightened reflexively.

"Put me down," she ordered after he'd gone a couple dozen yards. How could she be battling the urge to lean in and kiss his neck at the same time as feeling so childlike in their antics? "You've proved your point."

She might have worried that she was too heavy for him to carry, but he wasn't huffing or puffing or straining in the slightest. Which added *dainty* to the list of things he was making her feel. Had she ever felt dainty?

Laughing, Justin kept on jogging, his hands securely holding her legs at his waist. "Hang on and let me make it to the bridge. Man card on the line, remember?"

His man card had never been on the line. She knew exactly how manly he was—was haunted by memories of his manliness. And he sure wasn't laboring to carry her, which was a testament to how in shape he was.

Looking ahead, Riley eyed the bridge. It wasn't that far away, and he was making good headway in its direction.

"Okay. Since Daisy has hushed, and you seem determined to do this, to the bridge it is. Can't have your man card being revoked on my account."

"Phew, thank goodness for that."

"No one would believe this," she mused.

She didn't believe it. Who'd have thought earlier today that she'd be riding on Justin's back?

"Take a picture for proof?" he suggested, giving her leg a squeeze.

"Yeah, right. A picture of this—that's what I want. *Not.*"

"*I* want one," he surprised her by saying. "Take one for me. I bet we look cute."

"'Cute' is not the word I'm thinking."

Being careful to hold on with one arm around his neck, she dug into the pocket at her waist to pull out her phone. She didn't want a photo of them, but… But he said he did, so it would be rude not to take one, right?

He slowed to a stop as she held the phone up high, trying to get them at a decent angle.

"Here, let me."

Riley tightened her legs at his waist as he took her phone, held it farther out in front of them.

"Say cheese."

"Cheese!" she said, keeping her smile in place.

"Hmm, I couldn't get Daisy in," he said, holding the camera up again. "Let me try from a side angle." He snapped a couple more shots, then surprised her further by saying, "Now a silly one."

Even though she knew he couldn't see her face, she arched a brow. "As opposed to our non-silly ones?"

"Humor me?"

"I'm on your back, aren't I?"

He laughed. "That you are. Now, make a funny face."

She let go of his neck, held her arms out wide to her sides, kept her legs tight at his waist, and stuck her tongue out at her phone.

He clicked the screen a few times, then, laughing, pulled the photo up on her phone."Hey, that's great," he said.

He held it up to where she could see.

"I hope the others are better, because there's nothing 'great' about that one." Although she had to admit seeing Justin's face contorted into his "silly" pose did warm something inside her.

Or maybe that was just the trapped heat accumulating between their sweaty bodies.

He swiped his finger across the phone screen and showed her the next picture.

"This one is good."

He was right. The photo on the screen was perfect. Justin's face was full of good humor as he smiled at the camera, his eyes twinkled, and the sheen of sweat outlined his muscular arms perfectly. Her own smile looked real, relaxed, and her eyes sparkled. Even her skin glowed.

Must be the South Carolina humidity he'd mentioned, she thought. Because if she admitted it was the man she'd have a lot of soul-searching to do.

He handed the phone to her. "You'll have to send me these."

She slid it back into her pocket without taking another look, although she knew she'd painstakingly go through all the photos later. She wouldn't be able to resist. Just as she seemed unable to resist anything Justin dangled her way.

"Just so long as you don't show anyone," she said.

Why she'd added the caveat she wasn't sure. It had just come out. Maybe as a protest against how he pulled her out of her comfort zone. Maybe because her heart was still pounding like crazy at seeing the photos, at how they looked like a "real" couple, at how happy she looked.

In both photos her face glowed with something that had been missing for a long time. Happiness. But her smiles in the pictures shouldn't impress her. They were just reflections of who she was: a woman content with her life—right?

Justin tightened his hold on her legs, then resumed his progress toward the bridge, almost as if he thought she was going to tell him to put her down again. She should. His carrying her was just childishness.

"Why don't you want me to show the pictures to anyone?" he asked. "Are you ashamed for people to know you were with me?"

Her stomach twisted. "It's not that." She scrambled for a reason. "It would just give the wrong impression."

"What wrong impression would that be?"

"That we're involved."

Another hesitation, then, "Aren't we?"

Riley closed her eyes. She was surrounded by Justin. He was filling all her senses. His smell, his strength, the sound of his breathing as he carried her the short distance to the bridge, the feel of his muscles working against her body...

"Life will be simpler if we aren't." The exposed honesty of her admission shocked her.

The fact that he didn't push her to elaborate shocked her even more.

Reaching the bridge, he relaxed his hold on her legs and Riley slid off his back.

When she was on her feet, Justin turned. "Anytime you want to be carried rather than going it alone, just let me know."

Rather than answer him, or any of the questions swirling through her mind, Riley scooped Daisy up into her arms and took off, tossing over her shoulders, "Race you to the end."

Justin was smart enough to know that Riley had hoped he'd take off and leave her when she'd issued her challenge. She'd certainly picked up her pace from their earlier jogging. But he knew she wasn't trying to win a race. She just wanted to make conversation difficult.

He was okay with that. Maybe he even needed a moment to gather his wits after holding her. He wasn't sure he'd ever be able to touch Riley without feeling his blood heat. Holding her, even on their juvenile piggyback ride, had sent his insides into an adrenaline rush.

Her legs around his waist had given him instant flashbacks of a far more erotic wrapping of those long legs around him. Had sent him into an instant longing to take her back to his place and explore those legs at his leisure. To explore all of her. Her body and her mind, too.

He wanted to know what made her tick…what made her who she was. He'd learned a lot today. But he wanted to know more. Lots more. *Everything*, he admitted. He wanted to know everything there was to know about Riley.

And with time, he would.

Because, whether she wanted to or not, Riley liked him. She had admitted she didn't want to, which was maybe progress in getting her past whatever made her think she shouldn't. Surely, with patience, she'd realize liking him wasn't a problem? But her thinking she *shouldn't* like him, *shouldn't* want him, was a huge problem…

"By the way," she said now. "You didn't happen to find a gold cross on a chain?"

He glanced toward her. "No. Did you lose one?"

She nodded. "At some point over the past few days. I'd thought it might be in your Jeep or—well, you know…"

"I haven't seen one, but I haven't looked. It has sentimental value?"

"It was a gift."

"From a man?"

"From my mother," she corrected. "She gave it to me for my graduation. That I've lost it breaks my heart." Her voice broke as she made the admission.

"We'll check the Jeep when we get back to the parking area. Maybe we'll find it."

Please let it be here. Please let it be here.

Riley ran her hands around the edge of the passenger seat, checking beneath it. Nothing.

"It's not here."

"I'm sorry, Riley. I'd hoped it would be so I could play hero and give it back."

"If you found my necklace I'd definitely think you were a hero."

He turned back to the Jeep. "Let's look some more."

She shook her head. "Wishing isn't going to make it suddenly appear."

Still, he checked over everything on the passenger side one more time.

"Thanks for checking, though."

"You're welcome. I'll look when I get home and give you a call if I find it."

"I— Okay, that would be great."

"I'll need your number." He studied her. "Is that okay?"

"I— Sure. I guess so."

"If you hand me your phone, I'll dial mine. That way you can send me those pictures."

"That's fine."

She took her phone from around her waist, but didn't hand it over. Couldn't hand it over.

"Riley…?"

Taking a deep breath, she thrust the phone his way. "Here. Just take it and get it done."

Staring at her a bit oddly, he punched in his number and hit "dial." His phone began ringing. He pressed the stop button, then handed her phone back.

"Now, no excuses. Call me anytime."

Riley slid her phone back into the pouch. She wouldn't be calling Justin. He was much too dangerous to her sanity and well-being for her to have anything more to do with him.

"Come on, Daisy," she said to the dog. "Let's go home."

Justin sought Riley the moment he entered the operating room. Funny how, when everyone was dressed in the same surgical scrubs and protective wear, his gaze still went to her in instant recognition, as if he felt her presence as much as saw it.

The surgical crew today was identical to the previous day's. That didn't always happen, but Justin liked this group. They worked well together.

"Good morning, Dr. Brothers," Sheila greeted him.

"It *is* a good morning," he echoed.

"Somebody is in a lot better mood than he was yesterday," the anesthesiologist teased. "Feeling lucky?"

Justin forced his gaze not to go toward Riley, to see how she'd taken the doctor's comment.

"I'm lucky every day," he countered as he allowed a nurse to assist him in putting on his personal protection equipment.

"Hear, hear!" the anesthesiologist cheered.

"Lucky in cards. Lucky in lottery tickets. Lucky in races." With the last, Justin gave in and glanced toward Riley to see if his words had got a reaction.

"Remind me to have you to scratch off my next lottery ticket," she piped up, without looking up from the surgical tray she was inventorying.

Relieved that she'd joined in the conversation, he nodded. "Sure thing. I'll even let you borrow my lucky rabbit's foot if you want."

"Ew!" She glanced up, her eyes twinkling. "Please tell me you don't really have a rabbit's foot."

"Yeah, that would be gross, Dr. Brothers," Sheila added.

"Agreed—and I was speaking metaphorically. The only lucky foot I have is attached to the rest of me, and I've got two of them." He winked at Riley. "You're welcome to borrow one or both, though."

"I'm good," she countered. "Thanks, anyway."

"Better luck next time," the anesthesiologist put in.

Justin felt he'd been lucky *this* time. Riley's eyes had been expressive, had connected with his, and some warmth had passed between them.

She hadn't completely shut him out after the day before. He'd wondered if she would when her only response after he'd texted her that he hadn't found her necklace had been: Thanks for looking.

Lord, how he wished he'd been able to find it and give it back to her, and erase the sadness he'd seen when she'd told him about losing it.

Surgical cap, lighted visor with face shield, mask, gloves, shoe covers, protective apron over the operating room scrubs he'd donned just prior to coming into the surgical suite—all in place.

Justin stepped over to his anesthetized patient and gave his complete attention to the sleeping woman. "Cynthia Gibbons, sixty years old, left hip replacement," he began, and each member of the crew kicked into their professional role to make sure every aspect of Mrs. Gibbons's surgery went smoothly.

During the next two hours Justin worked, often chatting with the crew about whatever topic they happened to be on. Riley joined in. It almost felt like old times. Almost, but in some ways better.

Physically, she wound his insides tight…made him want what they'd had the night of Paul and

Cheyenne's party. Not just the sex, but the easy flow between them.

Although he wanted the sex, too.

Desperately.

Giving himself a little shake, he pushed Riley from his mind and focused on the joint he was repairing. When he'd finished he straightened, and stretched out his spine and shoulders.

"Great job," he praised his team.

His gaze once again went to Riley and their eyes met. She'd been looking at him.

He was surprised when she didn't immediately look away. Instead her eyes sparkled with tiny green flames that burned holes right through him.

Plus—although it might just be the bright lights shining above the operating table—he'd swear that beneath her scrub mask she was smiling.

At him.

He caught himself whistling twice that afternoon, getting more than a few eyebrow-raises from his coworkers.

But later, when he went back to the recovery area, planning to find Riley, he was disappointed to find she'd already gone.

So much for his belief that she was coming around to his way of thinking…

Riley didn't see Justin for the next couple of days as he wasn't on the OR schedule but working in clinic.

That didn't keep her from thinking about him. Nor did it keep her from looking at the photos he'd taken of them when she'd been riding piggyback.

Even though he'd asked her to, she'd not sent them to him. Something about sharing the pictures made her feel vulnerable—as if she would be giving him a part of herself, a part she needed to protect.

Stretched out on a hammock beneath two palm trees, she fiddled with her phone, flipping through the shots he'd taken, unable to keep herself from smiling. When she came to the one of their "silly" faces, she even snickered.

"What's so funny?" Cassie asked, plopping down on the hammock next to Riley and almost flipping them out as she sat on the edge, her feet barely touching the ground.

"Nothing." Face heating, Riley clicked her phone off as if she'd been caught looking at something naughty.

"Nothing?" Cassie asked, then shook her head. "You're not fooling me, you know."

Holding her phone close to her chest, Riley asked, "About what?"

Cassie rolled her eyes. "Why don't you just admit that you like him?"

"Who?"

From where she perched on the hammock, Cassie gave her the evil eye.

Riley sighed. "So I like him."

"What are you going to do about it?"

Good question.

"I'm not planning to do anything," she admitted, toying with her phone.

"Well, that's a crying out loud shame—because he likes you, too."

"How do you know?" *Eek.* That had been a lot of interest in her voice. Too much.

"You mean other than I saw how you two were eyeballing each other at Cheyenne and Paul's party?"

Riley sucked in a deep breath. "He's easy to look at. I'm not blind."

"If you don't see how he looks at you then you must be."

"How does he look at me?" She cringed because she'd asked, but she hadn't been able to stop the immediate question. Nor could she stop the way she waited with bated breath for her friend's answer.

"As if he wants to eat you up."

"That was just at Cheyenne and Paul's party… because we'd drunk a little too much."

"It's every time he's in the same room with you. It's been that way from the beginning."

Riley clicked her phone back on, pulled up the photos and handed the phone to Cassie.

Her friend's dark eyes widened. "When were these taken?"

"The other night when I took Daisy for a run. I bumped into him."

Cassie flipped through the photos. "You were having fun?"

Staring at the phone in her friend's hand, Riley shrugged. "I was."

"Justin looks like he was, too."

"He was." And if she hadn't already known, looking at the photos would have assured her that he had been.

"So what does this mean? And don't lie to me the way you keep lying to yourself."

Riley rubbed at her temples, started to say it meant nothing, but wasn't sure that was the truth. She *was* lying to herself, wasn't she?

"I wish I knew."

Cassie's expression softened. "Let me ask a different way. What do you *want* it to mean?"

"Justin says he wants to date me."

Still holding the phone, Cassie gave an excited squeal. "Then date the man! It's not as if he isn't a handsome, successful orthopedic surgeon who's a great guy and just happens to turn you on."

"There is that," Riley agreed, taking her phone back.

After watching her in silence for a few moments, Cassie asked, "Does this have to do with Johnny?"

"Ugh…" Now her temples really hurt. "Do we have to say his name out loud?"

"We don't have to. But since he's what's holding you back, we need to."

"He quit holding me back the moment he didn't show up for our wedding."

"Best thing that man ever did for you."

"True." She shuddered at the thought that had he shown up she would have tied herself to him for life. "I don't want to go through that again."

Cassie reached out and hugged Riley. "Johnny didn't deserve you. He never did. What he did to you on what was supposed to be the happiest day of your life was unforgivable. But it wouldn't happen again."

Trying not to cry, Riley inhaled and then blew out slowly. "You're right—because I won't let it."

She was content with her life, didn't need a man to be happy. But Justin...

Cassie gave her another squeeze. "It's been over a year, Riley."

"Not nearly long enough to forget what happened," she admitted, hugging her friend back, then pulling away.

"Don't forget it, but don't let it dictate your future," Cassie advised. "You deserve to be happy. And Justin makes you happy. If you don't believe me look at those pictures."

Cassie had left with Sam, but Riley stayed outside, lying in the hammock, enjoying the cool breeze. Daisy was curled in her lap and hadn't budged since a few minutes after Cassie had left. For that matter Riley barely had.

Reaching for her necklace to toy with the cross, she recalled too late that it wasn't there. Tears prickled her eyes. How *could* she have lost her necklace? She'd searched everywhere she could think of, had called around, and no one had found it—including Justin.

Justin. He was never far from her mind.

She picked up her phone and yet again looked at the photos that filled her with an equal mixture of confusion and joy. She should send them to him. He'd given her his number and she'd told him she would.

She glanced at the time. She'd been out longer than she'd thought. He'd been in surgery early that morning. He was probably asleep.

She'd been in surgery just as early and *she* wasn't sleeping, her nagging voice pointed out.

Pulling up his phone number, she attached the pictures and typed a message.

Here these are. Sorry it took me so long.

Before she could change her mind she hit Send, then closed her phone and stared up at the stars dotting the night sky and peeking through the trees.

Almost immediately her phone dinged, indicating a new message.

Thanks.

Her pulse went crazy, obviously thinking it

was going for some world record. Hands a little shaky, she typed...

You're welcome.

You in bed?

She should be in bed. *With him*, that nagging voice added. Riley grimaced and answered him.

No. Outside stargazing. You?

Same.

His answer surprised her. She typed again.

What?

I'm on my balcony, looking at the stars and letting go of the day's stress.

Bad day?

Not really. Just missed seeing you.

She closed her eyes. She'd missed seeing him, too.

Part of me wants to say that the day isn't over.

Even as she admitted it she surprised herself—and no doubt him. She was playing with fire and was going to get burned.

He messaged back.

I like that part of you. You should listen to it more often.

Despite her misgivings, Riley smiled.

You think?

I'd be there faster than you'd believe if you invited me.

I want to…but I won't.

I was afraid of that.

Don't be mad.

I'm not. I don't understand your reasons, but I do get that this isn't easy on you.

But it should be, shouldn't it? She bit into her lower lip. Should she try to explain her reasons to Justin? Really, it wasn't any of his business. Despite what had happened, they weren't dating.

He was texting again:

Giving in to one's desires? Easy as pie.

Are we talking dessert or the numerical pie? For the record, I never was good at math, so if you want to impress me, better make it dessert.

Why was she being flippant? Because she didn't want to discuss her reasons for being so afraid to give in to all the things she wanted to do with Justin? Because she was afraid? Or because she'd learned better than to take that risk when Johnny stood her up?

Any flavor you want. Just name it.

Sighing with a mixture of wistfulness and resignation at how Justin tempted her, Riley typed back.

I'll have to think on that one. Night, Justin.

Night, Riley. Text me if you change your mind. We could stargaze together.

Struggling with a mixture of giddy anticipation and leeriness, Riley reread her messages, typed some words…

Bring Key Lime!

Doing so made her smile even when she knew she'd never send them.

That was when it hit her. Prior to last Saturday she'd have thought Justin would have been out on a date. Never would she have assumed he'd be at home stargazing when he was off work the next morning.

She'd seen him with several different women over the months she'd known him. Why was he alone now? Had she misjudged him? Would a player really be alone on a Thursday night? Why was she so glad he was alone?

CHAPTER FIVE

"PLANS TODAY?"

Tell Justin yes, Riley ordered herself, even as she heard herself say rather sleepily into the phone that had just awakened her, "Nothing specific. Why?"

"I'm taking my Wilderness Group out on a kayaking trip in the Congaree National Park. One of the other adults canceled and I need a certain adult-to-child ratio."

Riley yawned and then, making sure not to disturb Daisy, who was curled next to her, rolled over in bed to look at her clock.

"I thought you might want to go," Justin continued.

"On a kayaking trip with your Wilderness Group?" She didn't even know what a Wilderness Group was.

"Nothing like a bunch of seven- and eight-year-olds floating down a river, right?"

"You've lost your mind."

He laughed at her comeback. "That means you want to go with me! I'd hate to disappoint the kids…"

Ugh. Justin was emotionally blackmailing her with the thought of seven- and eight-year-olds.

"How many kids are we talking about?"

"Nine signed up for the trip. I'm hoping they'll all show."

"You're taking *nine* kids out on the river?"

"They're great kids," he assured her. "Plus there'll be another adult there, and a guide."

Still, nine kids on a river… Sounded rather sketchy.

"You're sure it's safe?" Because she wasn't sure. They seemed too young.

"We'll have life jackets on the entire trip," he assured. "Besides, it's a slow float—not a white-water rafting trip. And the water isn't up as we've not had a lot of rain. We just need one more adult. Say you'll go."

"I'd be more a hindrance than help. Your seven- and eight-year-olds probably have more experience on a river than I do," she admitted. "I've never even been in a kayak."

"All the more reason for you to say yes. Experience something new. You'll have fun."

Maybe… Living in Columbia, she couldn't

drive around the city without passing over a bridge with a view of people enjoying the waterways in various ways. They always caught her eye with their colorful floats and kayaks.

"You don't even know if I can swim," she pointed out.

Her mother hadn't been able to swim, but Riley had learned during the hours she'd spent playing at the community center, after her mother had dropped her off for the day while she worked.

"Guess if you can't you'd better not fall out of your kayak…"

"Justin!"

He laughed. "I'm teasing. Do you think I'd risk you or my Wilderness Group getting hurt? It's a fun outing—a trip to get the kids outdoors, get some sunshine and see nature—not some kind of survival of the fittest training. I've taken them out before. Several times, actually. They're experienced on the water, they respect it, and like I said they'll be wearing life jackets at all times. I just need another adult present to keep my ratio of adult to kids correct."

She couldn't disappoint nine kids. Plus, being outdoors, getting some sunshine and seeing nature sounded heavenly. Still, she was only a mediocre swimmer, and she really had never been in a kayak or a canoe. She wouldn't be much help, surely?

"You're sure I wouldn't be in the way?"

"If you say no I may have to cancel. You won't be in the way. You'd be doing us a huge favor."

Indecision tugged at her. A day on the river with nine kids. A day on the river with Justin.

"There's no one else you can call?"

"At this last minute? You're my last hope."

Justin's last hope or ruin nine kids' day? When she didn't have anything better planned than catching up on her laundry and doing some yard work.

"Fine," she agreed, feeling a weight lift from her when she did so. Because of the kids. Not because she'd agreed to go out with Justin. At least that's what she assured herself. "I can't have a bunch of kids disappointed because I was too chicken to float down a river."

"That's the spirit," he encouraged, merriment evident in his voice. "And that's the way to keep from disappointing a grown man who wants to float down a river with you today, too."

"You say that *now…*" Climbing out of bed, she looked at the lazily stretching dog. "A couple of quick questions: what do I wear and what do I need to bring with me?"

"Wear clothes you don't mind getting wet. A bathing suit with T-shirt and shorts over it is ideal. Swimmer's shoes. Bring a water bottle. Bring dry clothes to change into afterward. I'll take care of everything else."

"Can I bring Daisy?"

"The boys would like that. Let me see if I can rustle up a life jacket for her."

"Seriously?"

She'd been mostly kidding when she'd asked, so his offer surprised her. Who knew they made life jackets for dogs? Or that Justin would not only humor her but be concerned for Daisy's safety?

"Would it make you happy to bring her?"

Riley glanced down at the dog, looking up at her with her big dark eyes set in her cute, fuzzy white face. "Yes, as long as it's safe for her, it would."

"Then, yes, I'm serious. I want you happy, Riley."

It was a fitting statement for him to make, given her and Cassie's conversation on Thursday. Justin wanted her happy.

And if the smile on her face now was anything

to go by, she'd say he'd got his wish. Which seemed to answer a lot of the other questions she'd been struggling with since waking up in his bed. Before that, even.

She'd been stressing over what to do about Justin from the moment her gaze had connected with his and he'd smiled, stealing her breath, making her hormones surge and upsetting the balance of her well-orchestrated life.

Riley met up with Justin and the others at Three Rivers Park, where a rental company had their kayaks ready and waiting. Justin had his own kayak, with a small cooler strapped to the back and a smaller waterproof supplies box strapped to the front.

Once in the river, the kids began having a blast, pretending they were pirates and that Justin was their Captain.

"Is Daisy okay, Miss Riley?" asked Kyle, the youngest of the boys, from his kayak.

The sandy-haired child had an impish smile and dark brown eyes, and he seemed to have made it his mission to keep a check on Daisy, never rowing too far away from Riley's kayak.

Supposedly she was keeping an eye on Kyle and one other boy, Jevon, who also stayed close to her kayak without her saying a word. Perhaps Justin had asked them to keep tabs on her? She wouldn't put it past him.

She glanced at her dog, wearing the life jacket Justin truly had come up with and looking absolutely adorable. Daisy was perched in the kayak, surveying the water with great interest, but not enough to be tempted to dive in at any point. She seemed content with taking in the scenery. Fortunately Riley had kept her kayak afloat thus far, with no tip-overs, and she and Daisy hadn't taken any spills into the river.

All the same, Justin had hooked her to Riley, so that the dog couldn't get more than a few feet away even if she wanted to. Riley liked it that he'd thought of all these extra touches to keep Daisy safe, and knew he'd done the same, likely much more, for the boys.

"Yeah, I think Daisy is feeling on top of the world," she told Kyle. "This life being captured by pirates doesn't seem to bother her."

Daisy was probably getting a big head with all the attention she was receiving from the kids—Kyle especially. The boys had been so excited to meet her, even if Daisy only looked at them as if they were crazy when they tried to get her to do tricks. Daisy's one and only trick was to sit, and she only did that when she wanted—which wasn't often.

The boy paddled his kayak closer and held on to the side of Riley's, keeping their crafts side-by-side as they floated along the gently moving river. Although there had been a few sections of water that her required paddling, they could have floated most of the trip like this, without any work other than making sure they didn't run ashore or run into the rare downed tree.

"Could have" being the key phrase. Because the boys weren't content with a leisurely float and were only happy if they were paddling. If not for the guide slowing them down to point out various turtles, birds, and other wildlife, they'd probably have already finished their trek.

"Captain Brothers didn't really kidnap you, did he?" Kyle asked, his expression telling her that he hero-worshipped Justin more than a little and wouldn't believe anything negative she said.

Smiling, Riley shook her head. "Shh, don't let the others know, but Daisy is the only real princess you guys are holding captive."

Kyle grinned. "I didn't think so. Captain Brothers is too nice."

"Pirate captains aren't usually nice, are they?" Riley couldn't resist teasing the boy.

"Captain Brothers is," Kyle assured her. "He's a *nice* pirate."

"That he is," Riley agreed—although she wasn't too sure about the pirate part. The more she learned about Justin, the more she admired him, and questioned her initial impression of him as a playboy.

Which didn't mean anything except that he was a good guy. Good guys existed. Who knew?

"Are you Captain Brothers's girlfriend?"

At Kyle's question Riley's face heated—and not because of the hot South Carolina sunshine. "No." *Not even close.* "We work together at the hospital."

In the way that impish little boys did, Kyle grinned. "Maybe you can be *my* girlfriend."

Not sure what to say, and certainly not wanting to encourage him, but knowing he'd meant the comment as a compliment, Riley smiled, part of her flattered that he'd do so. "Maybe... But I'm betting that when you grow up you'll have lots of much younger girlfriends."

With a cheeky grin, Kyle waggled his brows. "I have lots of girlfriends now."

"You rascal," she teased, wondering at what age boys even started having girlfriends, much less lots of them. Seven seemed young. Still, what did she know about kids? And Kyle was adorable and seemed so proud of his claim. "A girlfriend in each port, eh? You really are a pirate."

He beamed. "Captain Brothers says I'm his first mate."

There went another big dose of that hero-worship.

"That must mean you're special. Daisy sure thinks so."

The boy's grin widened.

"Kyle? Are you making sure Miss Riley isn't planning an escape?" Justin called from where he floated behind the group.

Both Riley and Kyle twisted to look behind them at the man they'd been discussing. Riley couldn't see Justin's eyes behind his dark sunglasses, but his smile was wide. She imagined his eyes were twinkling with mirth.

He'd stayed at the back the entire trip so far, saying he preferred to be where he could see all the kids and make sure no one got left behind or had any issues. The guide stayed in the front, leading their way down this somewhat shallow section of the Congaree River. Riley stayed near the back too, and Stan, the dad of a boy named Stephen, paddled in the middle of their small group.

Although Justin had said he needed her there, Riley wasn't so sure. One adult per three kids seemed a good enough ratio, although admittedly one adult to just over two kids was better. Not that she'd done anything other than help apply sunscreen to little faces and ears, and supervised as they'd applied it to other exposed body parts.

Honestly, after the length of time Justin had had to spend getting her and Daisy settled securely into their kayak, she was probably more of a hindrance than a help.

"Aye-aye, Captain!" Kyle called. "I'm questioning her."

"That he is!" Riley tried to hold in her laughter at Kyle's salute to Justin.

Kyle let go of her kayak and their boats separated. She expected him to row ahead. Instead he stuck close, pointing out a turtle sunning itself on the bank and talking to her about everything from baseball to his favorite video game.

When they reached the place where the guide had stopped, ready for their lunch break, Riley stayed back until Justin had gotten out of his kayak, then watched him help a few of the boys pull their kayaks up on the bank so they wouldn't go floating away. She wasn't exactly sure how to get out of hers without tipping the kayak over—which she'd rather not do.

"I'll take Daisy," Kyle offered, wading out in the water to where Riley was trying to watch how the others were getting out of their kayaks. "That way she won't be scared of falling in when you get out."

"Good idea," Riley agreed, and unhooked Daisy's lifejacket from hers, and handed the dog to Kyle. At least if she tipped the kayak Daisy wouldn't get dumped into the water.

Once Kyle had Daisy, Riley contemplated again how to get out of the kayak. The kids had made it look easy enough, but every time she shifted her weight the boat tilted.

"Need a hand?" Justin offered, smiling down at her.

"Or two or three hands," she admitted, taking his outstretched one to balance herself as she attempted to get out of the kayak.

With him steadying her, she managed to land with her feet in the water rather than her rear-end.

"Oh, that's cold!" she exclaimed as the calf-deep water soaked her tennis shoes. Justin had told her to wear swimming shoes, but she didn't own a pair. These old tennis shoes had had to suffice.

"Feels good," Justin claimed, holding her hand and keeping the other on the rope attached to her kayak to keep it from floating away.

The sun was shining down hot on them, but goosebumps prickled Riley's skin as she climbed ashore to join the others. From the cold water or from where Justin held her hand?

"Feels good if you're a polar bear," she mumbled as she carefully made her way through the river to the bank. "Thank you," she added, once they were on dry land.

Letting go of her hand to pull her kayak up on the shoreline, next to the others, he grinned. "You're welcome. Can't have my favorite girl taking a swim before the designated time. I'd have a revolt, with lots of boys diving in under the pretext of rescuing you."

Rather than answer she just smiled, and made her way over to where Kyle was cuddling Daisy. Once there, she glanced back toward where Stan and the guide had begun unloading the things bungee-strapped to their kayaks.

Justin's arms and face glistened in the sunlight with a deepening tan, and memories of his bare chest flashed through her mind. She didn't recall any tan lines on his arms, but there must have been. Next time she'd look closer...

Next time?

There would be no next time.

Justin laughed at something the guide had said and Riley's heart missed a beat. Face on fire, she dragged her gaze away from Justin's muscular arms and ordered her brain to never, *ever* go again where it had just been.

Fortunately Kyle, still holding a wiggling Daisy, wanted her attention.

"She wants to get down, Miss Riley, but I wasn't sure if I should let her," he told her, keeping a tight grip on the dog, who was doing her best to wrangle her way free.

Poor Kyle. Riley was impressed that he continued to hold on to Daisy, despite her escape attempts. Although only six pounds, Daisy could be a handful.

"It's probably best if we put on her leash since we're in a place that's strange for her," Riley told him.

She'd left the short cord that had attached their lifejackets to each other back in the kayak, but she had brought Daisy's leash with her in the fanny pack she'd filled with treats, her phone inside a sealed plastic bag, a small bottle of sunscreen, and a protective lip balm. Being careful not to dislodge any of the other items, she pulled out Daisy's leash.

"Does she need to leave her lifejacket on?" asked Kyle.

Riley nodded. "I don't think she'll go in the water, but let's leave it on just in case. I'll hook this to her collar and then you can let her down."

She attached the leash and Kyle set Daisy down—although it was more a case of Daisy leaping from his arms the moment he relaxed his hold.

Daisy sniffed the ground for a few seconds, but then, rather than run off, she got on her hind legs and danced around at Kyle's feet, making him laugh.

"She likes me," he said, bending to pet her and baby-talk to her before taking off toward the other boys when Justin called him.

"That she does," Riley agreed, walking behind Daisy as she sniffed rocks, grass, a few stray bushes, then pulled against her leash with a backward glance that said *Come on*. Riley let the leash out, and wasn't surprised when Daisy went to the outskirts of the group where they were resting. "Funny girl," Riley teased the dog.

When Daisy had finished her business she went back to the group and once again wanted to be the center of the boys' attention—which they eagerly supplied even though they were supposed to be listening to the guide talking about the Congaree National Park.

Not wanting to get the boys in trouble, Riley scooped up Daisy and stood beside Justin, listening to the brief talk about how the forest around them boasted the tallest specimens in the United States of at least fifteen different varieties of tree.

"Anything I can do to help?" she whispered to Justin when he moved away to start unpacking a cooler.

She wanted to be useful. Or maybe she just wanted an excuse to be near him, to watch him with the boys and marvel at this unexpected side to him.

Someday Justin was going to be a great dad.

The thought was like a punch to the uterus. Justin would be a great dad, but that was nothing to do with her. She didn't want it to be anything to do with her. She'd never be a mom—wouldn't risk failing a child the way her father had failed her. And after Johnny's betrayal she'd given up all thoughts of being a mother.

But she couldn't quite shake the image of a little boy with sparkly blue eyes, a quick grin, and his dad's dark sun-streaked hair...

"You being here is enough."

Justin was answering her question, unaware that her mind was casting him in a paternal role. Thank goodness!

"Just relax and enjoy the scenery," he said.

Not wanting to be in the way, and needing a moment to shake the image, Riley led Daisy to the water's edge to let her get a drink, then followed her as she explored their immediate vicinity.

Keeping a hold on Daisy's leash as the dog sniffed the ground near a wild rhododendron, Riley let her gaze go again to Justin. He was busy with the kids, leaving her free to watch from behind her sunglasses without worrying that he'd catch her.

The kids adored him. That much was easy to see. And no wonder. He knew each kid well, called them by their names, and obviously spent time with them on a regular basis.

Seeing him with them had brought to light the fact that there were a lot of things she didn't know about Justin. Other than that he was a great coworker, a fantastic orthopedic surgeon, a phenomenal lover, and that she enjoyed being around him.

Justin had motioned to the guide that he was ready, and the young man lined up the boys. Justin squirted sanitizer into their hands, then inspected them prior to letting the boys move along in their makeshift lunch line. Stan handed each kid a bagged-up sandwich, while the guide joined them and let each one pick a piece of fruit and a bag of chips. Each boy had their own water bottle with their name printed on it, which they'd had tied to their kayaks during their float and had removed at some point.

"All right, mateys—what do we do with our trash?" Justin gave the kids an expectant look that said they'd reviewed this often in the past.

"Bring it all with us," one said.

"Not leave any trace of it," another said.

"Eat it!" Stephen said, giggling, causing all the boys to burst into laughter and his dad to frown at him.

"Good answers," Justin praised, then eyed the giggling boy. "Except Stephen, who has to eat his trash or walk the plank." He winked at the kids. "The rest of you bag it up for us to take back with us."

"Yes, Captain Brothers!" they said in almost perfect unison, giggling as they said it.

Kyle tugged on Justin's sleeveless shirt, where it was poking out from beneath his lifejacket. "Stephen doesn't have to really eat his trash or walk the plank, does he?"

Justin laughed and rubbed the boy's head. "You think I should let him off the hook?"

Kyle nodded. "This one time, Captain."

Justin winked at the boy. "Guess we'll let him bag up his trash, too, then."

Kyle grinned. "Thanks, Captain."

"You're welcome." Justin returned his attention to the rest of the crew. "Now, you pirates— eat, cleanup after yourselves, stay where I can see you, and we'll be back on the river in thirty minutes, to plunder the rest of these waters for treasure."

When Daisy had thoroughly checked out her immediate surroundings, she eyed the boys who were gathering their food with longing, like the little scavenger she was.

"You can't have the boys' lunch," she warned the dog, but Daisy's expression said, *Yeah, right.*

Riley spotted an old log about twenty meters back from where the group was gathering for their lunch. Leading Daisy, she walked over to it, sat down on the log, and watched as Justin and the other two adults got the boys settled.

Even in this environment, where Justin was doing anything but trying to look sexy, Riley found him so. How could she not with the sunlight glinting off his hair, highlighting every natural hue? With his arm muscles perfectly displayed in his sleeveless T-shirt and lifejacket? With his easygoing rapport with the boys and how their eyes filled with adoration when they looked at him?

Ugh. She should not be finding his parenting skills sexy. His parenting skills were none of her business.

As if he sensed her thoughts were on him, he looked her way, grinned, then came over to her, held out the hand disinfectant.

"Can't have you picking up any germs on our trip," he teased, squirting a generous dollop into her palm. "I'd miss you if you had to call out of work."

She rubbed her hands together and held them out for his inspection, as the boys had.

He made a show of checking them. "Guess that'll do."

"Thanks, Captain," she replied, unable to resist the tease. "Good to know I pass muster."

His gaze met hers from behind his mirrored sunglasses and heat filled her at what shone in his face.

Lust and so much more.

Her insides trembled with the recall of what it had felt like to be the sole recipient of his attention.

She didn't need to hear his, "Oh, you pass muster, all right..." to know she wasn't the only one battling physical attraction.

CHAPTER SIX

RILEY DRAGGED HER gaze from Justin's face to what he held.

"Sandwiches are all the same, so I hope you like peanut butter and jelly."

"No problem. I know we captives can't be choosy. But are you sure you have enough for me to have one? I don't want to take anything away from the kids."

"I brought plenty for the kids—besides, even pirates' captives have to keep up their strength when they're expected to man their own ship."

"There is that." Her gaze dropped to the sandwich and her stomach growled. "I *am* hungry."

"Floating down the river works up an appetite."

Were they talking food or a different type of appetite? If so, the river had nothing to do with how starved she felt. Justin alone was responsible for the cravings rocking her.

Taking the sandwich and removing it from

the bag, she eyed him before taking a bite. "You know, when you said 'floating,' I pictured a relaxing trip, enjoying the scenery—not all this paddling to keep pace with the kids. They seem to think we're in a race to get to the end."

"They always do." He walked over to the makeshift lunch line and grabbed a sandwich of his own, some fruit, and a couple of individual-sized bags of chips.

Once back to where she sat, he joined her on the log. "Banana or apple?"

She took the apple and the bag of chips he held out. "Best sandwich ever. Thank you."

"Admit it," he said.

Taking another bite of her sandwich, she glanced toward him in question and purposely avoided looking at Daisy, who was expectantly waiting for a bite.

"You're glad you came," he clarified.

Chewing the bite she'd taken, she nodded. "Beats working in my yard any day of the week."

Even if her yard work wouldn't have left her wanting to wrap her arms around Justin's neck, to run her fingers through the damp hair at his nape and feel his lips against hers.

"What kind of yard work? I could help you," he offered.

Face warm, Riley avoided looking toward him. "Just cleaning up my landscaping, putting down some fresh mulch…that kind of thing. Why would you want to help with that?"

"You've helped me today," he reminded.

"This…" she waved her hand toward where the kids were sitting near the river, eating their lunches, with the two other adults sitting close, chatting about how great the weather was "…doesn't fall into the same category as yard work."

"Agreed, this is awesome, but I'd be glad to help you—especially since I've kept you from getting it done today."

She shook her head. "There's no rush. I'm just sprucing things up and doing some weeding and trimming."

"I could come later—or even tomorrow. With both of us working you'd get finished a lot quicker."

She eyed him from behind her sunglasses. "Did you just invite yourself to my house?"

He grinned a bit sheepishly. "Consider it more an offer of free labor."

Justin at her house. Doing her yard work. How

could she explain that she didn't want him there for fear that she'd invite him inside?

"I wouldn't feel right, having you over to work."

"What are friends for?"

What, indeed? And was that what they were? Friends? Riley didn't recall ever having any close male friends. Not even Johnny. She'd planned to marry him, so he should have been her friend, right? But she didn't recall ever thinking he was her friend.

Which probably should have clued her in that she shouldn't marry him.

Still, he'd been hardworking—or so she'd thought—handsome, and he had claimed to love her. She'd been reeling from her mother's death and had been easy pickings for the suave salesman.

What was her excuse with Justin?

Johnny wasn't fit to tie Justin's shoes.

"Riley?"

She blinked at Justin, knowing her last thought was true. "Hmm?"

"Just making sure you're okay. You got quiet."

"Enjoying my lunch."

Seeming to take her answer at face value, Justin stretched his legs out in front of the log. "It is nice, isn't it?"

She nodded, took another bite, and refused to think of what the conclusions she was drawing about the man next to her meant.

Besides, lunch *was* nice—as were their beautiful surroundings. Off in the distance she could see Columbia's skyline, and in the other direction lay the Congaree National Park. Gorgeous trees lined the river banks. The sky was a beautiful blue with the occasional dotting of a white puffy cloud. The sun was hot, but there was just enough of a breeze to make the day feel perfect.

The day *was* perfect.

"Beautiful," she said, and meant it.

They finished eating. Stephen's dad and five of the boys had waded into the water and were attempting to catch minnows. The guide had gone beyond the kayaks and was animatedly talking to someone on his cellphone. The other four boys were digging through rocks, looking for the fossils that they deemed highly valuable.

Spotting Daisy, Kyle came running over. "Can Daisy help us look for treasure?"

"Sure." Riley handed the leash over and watched him run off toward the other boys, Daisy in tow. "He is a cute kid."

"He is—although a bit of a Casanova, it seems."

Riley glanced toward a grinning Justin.

"I heard him ask you to be his girlfriend."

Riley waved off his teasing. "Sounds like Kyle has more than enough girls keeping him occupied currently."

"I hope so."

Wrinkling her brows at how serious his voice had grown, Riley glanced at Justin.

"Sorry. It's just that I doubt he has much of a chance to keep any girlfriend for long."

Wondering what he meant, Riley waited for him to continue. When he didn't, she asked.

"Kyle lives in foster care—has done on and off since he was two."

Riley's heart squeezed.

"All these boys do except Stephen," Justin continued.

"I didn't realize…"

She glanced out at the kids, watching them laugh and play. They looked so happy and carefree.

With further respect for the man next to her, she asked, "How did you get involved in their lives?"

"Long story short, Stephen is a bit accident-prone. Over the years I've reset a few broken bones. His dad and I hit it off. Three years ago he told me about how he wanted to do more, to provide good role models for foster kids. Knowing I wouldn't say no, he asked if I'd help start this group."

"Wow," she said, truly impressed.

Justin would have still been in residency back then. For him to have volunteered with any group during that busy time spoke volumes about the man and what he'd done with what little spare time he would have had.

How had she ever labeled him as a player?

Okay, so he had gone out with several women since she'd met him, but maybe he just hadn't found someone he wanted a long-term relationship with, and that was why it seemed he was always with a different woman at the social events they both attended.

"At least twice a month we take the boys out on an excursion of some kind," he continued. "We try to do outdoors adventures, as most won't have that opportunity otherwise. But sometimes we just go for pizza and to the movies or the arcade."

"How many kids are there in your group?"

"We have ten, but it's rare all ten make it to an outing. That we have nine today is good."

Guilt hit her that she didn't make better use with her time outside of work. "Is it still the same ten boys as in the beginning?"

He nodded. "Our goal is to try to make a difference in these boys' lives—to give them positive role models and to follow them through until they're adults."

"Great goals—and how lucky they are to have you in their lives."

Justin shrugged. "It's the other way around. I'm lucky to have *them* in my life."

He certainly seemed to enjoy being with the kids. Still, Riley knew it wasn't all fun and games to organize trips for ten kids. At least, she didn't imagine it was. Reality was she'd never organized a trip for *one* kid, much less ten.

"Why did you call it Wilderness Group?"

One side of Justin's mouth hiked up. "Would you believe it's because they're wild?"

She glanced at the playing boys, then gave Justin a skeptical look.

He laughed. "Stan came up with the name before we even officially formed the group. We needed to call it something, but we wanted a

name the boys would like being a part of—
something that was for them. Wilderness Group
sounds good to ten boys who are in and out of
foster homes because they have parents who
can't or won't take care of them."

Realizing what poor home lives they had,
Riley stared out at the kids as they balanced on
an old log, walking from one end to the other
with their arms held out to their sides.

"That breaks my heart for them."

Justin nodded. "Mine, too—which is another
reason I love doing this. For at least a couple
times a month they get to do fun, normal kid
things. Don't get me wrong—some of these
boys are in great foster homes—but they've all
known heartache none of them should have experienced."

Riley stared at him, amazed by the empathy
in his voice, the affection she could hear for the
boys. He truly cared about them and he was
willing to do something to make their lives better. She didn't know anything about Stan's fi-
nances, but she'd bet Justin funded the group's
activities without even thinking twice.

Because he was a giver rather than a taker.

Because he was so much better a man than
her own father had been.

Her father hadn't thought twice about abandoning Riley and her mother, much less tried to do anything to lessen their financial burden. Thank goodness Riley's mother had loved her so much and had been able to take on extra work to provide for them.

Reaching up to tug on her necklace, Riley let her hand fall away in disappointment as she recalled her missing necklace.

What would her mother think of Justin?

Now, where had *that* thought come from? What her mother would have thought of Justin didn't matter any more than it mattered that Riley's father had skipped out. He'd just been preparing her for life—for men like Johnny who'd come along and then leave her, too.

Was Justin even for real? And, if so, how was it that he wanted to date a slightly plump, jaded about love, nurse like her?

"Captain Brothers!" Kyle shrieked, just as a loud cry of pain filled the air.

Riley's throat tightened as she glanced toward the boys.

"Man down! Man down!" Kyle motioned for them to hurry.

Justin leapt from the log and took off toward where the boys were now huddled around Stephen, who was lying on the ground and holding his bent leg against his belly. Blood covered his hands.

Heart racing, Riley ran to where Stephen lay. Blood gushed down his leg from a jagged gash on his knee.

"Get the first aid kit out of my kayak," said Justin.

Riley rushed to the kayak and grabbed the first aid kit from inside the supplies box. When she got back to the boys, Justin had taken off his lifejacket and his shirt. He'd torn a strip from the bottom of his T-shirt, exposing a sliver of tanned belly, then made a makeshift tourniquet and was now tying it to Stephen's leg to slow the bleeding.

Riley opened the kit, grabbed some gloves for Justin, handed them to him.

Hoping to help, Riley gloved up, too, and opened a packet of gauze and disinfectant.

"Thanks," Justin told her as she bent down beside him and began applying pressure to the wound with the gauze.

"Stan, will you get the boys to pack everything back into the kayaks?"

With one last glance at his son, Stan nodded, knowing Justin was trying to occupy the other kids rather than have them surrounding Stephen. "Come on, guys, let's give the doc some room while we make sure we leave this place the way we found it."

The guide, realizing something had happened, had ended his phone call and come over to check on them. His face paled at the sight of the blood oozing down Stephen's leg. It had slowed significantly with the makeshift tourniquet but hadn't completely stopped.

Wondering if the guide was going to pass out, Riley looked at him and gestured to the boys. "Maybe you could help the others?"

With one last look at the bleeding leg, the young guide nodded, then went over to where Stan had the boys searching for stray bits of trash in a game of seeing who could find the most.

Justin and Riley worked to clean Stephen's gaping cut, rinsing it with saline to make sure there was no stray debris or germs.

"Needs sutures," Riley observed, hating the pain that showed on Stephen's contorted face. Still, the boy was being a trouper.

Justin nodded, called Stan over. "Looks like we're going to be upping the scar count."

"Does that mean you're sewing me?" Stephen asked, tears streaking his face.

Giving the boy an empathetic look, Justin nodded. "I think so, buddy."

"I figured you'd need to when I saw how much he was bleeding." Stan sighed, then bent next to his son to kiss the top of his head. "It'll be all right. The doc is going to take care of you."

Not looking thrilled at the prospect, Stephen nodded nonetheless, as if he had already had this done repeatedly and knew the drill.

"I appreciate it," Stan told Justin, shaking his head. "Saves us from another run to the emergency room." Turning to Riley, he added, "Dr. Brothers has sutured this kid on three different occasions. He thought I'd asked him to help with the group because I needed another adult, but really it was just to have an on-site physician for my kid."

Stan patted his son's shoulder. Stephen had stopped crying, but his poor face was tear-stained and dirt-streaked.

His eyes were puffy and red as he told Riley, "I'm accident-prone."

"Just a little," Justin teased. "You ready for this, big guy?"

Wincing, and appearing to brace himself for

what was to come, Stephen took his dad's hand and then nodded.

Doing one last thorough wash and inspection of the gash, Justin turned to Riley. "There's a vial of anesthetic and a syringe in there. Will you draw me up three milliliters?"

Riley did so, then changed the needle over to a small gauge and handed it to Justin.

He squirted some of the numbing liquid into the open wound, waited a few seconds and then, moving through the wound, began anesthetizing the area.

Dabbing the gash every so often, Riley kept the blood from obscuring the wound so that Justin could see it.

"Grab that suture kit and open it for me, please."

Riley got the kit, opened it, and held out the small packet while trying to maintain a sterile field the best she could on a riverbank, while also dabbing the wound to clear away the blood.

When Justin had the needle held in the needle holder Riley patted the area. Then, balancing the kit on her thigh, she pushed the edges of the cut together as best as she possibly could to make Justin's work easier.

"Thanks," he said as he pushed the needle

through one side of the cut and then curved it around to come out on the other. He pulled it through, then began tying knots, wrapping the Ethilon in opposite directions with each loop. When he'd made several ties, he snipped the thread, then put in the next suture.

The cut was jagged and ended up requiring seven sutures to close it. When he'd finished the last one, Riley wet a piece of clean gauze and began cleaning dried blood from around the laceration.

"Nice work, Dr. Brothers." Despite his crude work area the sutures were perfectly placed, and the wound should heal nicely.

"Thanks. Stephen keeps me in practice—don't you, bud?"

Not that he didn't get plenty of practice in surgery, Riley thought, but kept her mouth closed.

"He's a trouper, for sure," the boy's father praised.

"'Cause I know the drill," Stephen informed them, looking up at them. "Do pirates have lots of scars, Captain Brothers?"

"Usually three or four, so you're good," Justin assured him as he removed the T-shirt strip from the boy's leg, watching the closed wound to make sure the bleeding didn't restart.

When it didn't, he turned to Riley. "Thanks for the assistance, Nurse Riley. We're going to have to either set you free or officially have you join the crew as an honorary medic. Which is it going to be?"

"Hmm..." She pretended to be considering his offer. "I may have to think on this one. Captive or honorary medic... Decisions, decisions..."

Having finished gathering the trash and stored all their belongings properly in their kayaks, the boys had come over to make sure Stephen was okay.

Kyle patted Riley's leg. "Being a pirate is a lot of fun."

"Says the kid with no ulterior motive!" Justin teased.

"Kyle just likes Daisy, right?" She smiled at the boy as she picked up all the pieces of dirty gauze, then turned her gloves inside out as she took them off, capturing the gauze inside.

"Daisy is pretty cool. When I grow up I'm going to have a dog, too."

Not as a child, though—unless one of his foster families happened to have one, and then he'd have to say goodbye to it whenever his time was up with that particular family.

Riley's heart squeezed at that reality. How many homes had Kyle been in over the years?

She fought the desire to hug the boy to her. Although he seemed a bit smitten with her, she didn't think he'd appreciate any show of affection in front of his friends.

That she even wanted to hug him surprised her. She'd never been around kids much—mostly felt uncomfortable when she was. The fact that she'd come today, was enjoying being with the boys and felt a connection to them was shocking.

Perhaps it was because she felt a kind of affinity with them? Because she understood what it felt like to have a parent abandon you.

"Is Stephen going to be okay?" the guide asked.

"He'll be fine. He has a lot of accidents and Captain Brothers always fixes him," Kyle piped up, before any of the adults could answer. "When I grow up I'm going to be a pirate captain doctor who has a dog!" the boy announced, and then, carefully holding on to the dog's leash, told Daisy to come on.

Riley watched him skip off, happy as could be and unfazed by what had happened to Stephen. Unfazed by *anything* that had happened to him up to that point in his life, or giving a good impression of it.

In the meantime Stan had helped his son up off the ground and was holding his hand as Stephen tried walking. The boy limped a bit, with a few grimaces, but had no real difficulties. Father and son went off to get ice from the cooler to put on the area.

"What's his story?" Riley asked as they walked away.

"Kyle's or Stephen's?"

She'd meant Kyle, but realizing Stephen must have a story, too, she felt her heart quicken. "Both."

"Stan and his wife adopted Stephen when he was four. He'd been in a dozen or so foster homes, but no one wanted to keep him because of all his accidents."

"That sounds ominous. Just how many accidents has he had?"

"During his lifetime?" Justin shrugged. "Hundreds, I imagine, based on what I know from the past few years."

"Why?"

"He has poor balance and he trips easily. His pediatrician isn't sure if it's from the drugs his mother stayed on while she was pregnant with him or if he suffered shaken baby syndrome or some other ailment. They haven't been able to pinpoint any specific abnormality that's causing the issue—they just know that he has balance and coordination issues, which leads to a lot of accidents for an active kid."

Watching Stan check on Stephen's gashed knee, his eyes full of love and concern for the boy, Riley mused, "I didn't realize Stephen was adopted."

"Stan and his wife fell in love with him during his stay with them as a foster kid. Fortunately they have great medical insurance, and the courts agreed Stephen was better off with them than in state custody."

"Thank goodness."

Justin nodded. "Stephen got lucky. Most of these kids aren't ever released from their birth parents long enough to be available for adoption. The ones who *are* released are often too old to be wanted by the time their birth parents sign over their rights. Most end up going from one foster family to another, with occasional time spent with their birth mother or father in between until they lose custody again."

Riley grimaced. "That's terrible."

Justin nodded.

"I wish I could bring them all home with me," Riley mused, not sure what she'd do with a bunch of boys, but knowing she'd smother them with love.

The knowledge stunned her. Johnny hadn't wanted kids and she'd agreed. Having been a child put through the agony of losing a parent had left her thinking she'd rather not, so going along with him had been easy.

Maybe because she'd never trusted that Johnny wouldn't leave.

Justin's gaze cut to her and he grinned at what she'd said. "Better not let Kyle hear you say that. He might offer to grant your wish. Rumor has it that his birth mother plans to sign away her rights and he'll be available for adoption."

How could someone not want a kid as precious as Kyle? "She's giving him away?"

"Honestly, since she's unable to take care of him, it's the best thing she could do for him. I can't imagine it's an easy decision for her or any parent, though." Justin's face tightened a little. "Kyle's not been back with her for over a year and has only seen her once during that time."

Riley couldn't imagine that giving up parental rights would be an easy decision. Nor could she imagine not seeing her own child more than once during a year's time. But maybe it wasn't nearly as difficult as she thought, since her own father had had no issue with walking away andnever looking back.

Kyle had no stability and apparently he never had. And he had a mother who didn't want him or wanted him but couldn't provide care for him.

Riley preferred to think it was the latter. Maybe because it was what she'd always wanted to believe of her father. That he hadn't left because he hadn't wanted her, but that he hadn't been able to take care of her and her mother.

She'd never believed it. Maybe in Kyle's case it was true, though…

"Is his foster family planning to adopt him?" She hoped that, like Stephen, Kyle would find a family to love him.

Justin's eyes darkened a little and he started to say something, then changed his mind. "Not that I'm aware of. They're nice people, with two grown kids of their own, and have been taking in foster children for about ten years now."

Riley had grown up without her father, but her mother had always been there, had always wanted and loved her. Not once had she ever felt alone or unloved as a child.

Just as an adult.

Now, where had *that* come from? She was not unloved as an adult. But the truth was since her mother's death she hadn't felt connected to any other person than her friend Cassie.

She'd wanted to be—acknowledged that her engagement to Johnny, and her unwillingness to see what had been so obvious, had mostly been about that desire to love and be loved. But she'd looked in all the wrong places.

Maybe, despite knowing how much her mother had loved her, the fact that her father hadn't stung more than she'd ever admitted.

Maybe she had more in common with the boys than she'd thought.

"I want to be a pirate."

At her blurted comment, Justin raised his brows. "Really?"

"Can I join your club?"

Because the more she thought about it, the more she knew she needed to be a part of these kids' lives. On the surface, it was for them, but the reality was she needed to be involved for *her*—to make a difference in their lives the way her mother had in hers.

"Are women allowed?"

"Allowed and welcomed," he assured her, looking pleased. "The more the merrier. And you wouldn't be the sole female. Stan's wife would have been here today except something came up last-minute with one of their other foster children. You took her place."

"They still foster children even after adopting Stephen?" She wasn't sure why that surprised her—maybe because of all his accidents—but the fact that they did made her happy. "How many do they have?"

"Currently they have one birth child and two foster children in addition to Stephen."

Looking around at the group, already seemingly completely recovered after Stephen's accident, probably because it was par for the course, Riley felt warmth fill her.

"Thank you for inviting me. Today has been a very good day."

"It has, hasn't it?" Justin grinned as he reached out and gave her hand a gentle squeeze. "And the best part is that it's not over."

CHAPTER SEVEN

JUSTIN WISHED RILEY had let him pick her up from her place that morning. That way he'd have had an excuse to spend more time with her. As it was, she'd driven herself, and he needed to wait at Three Rivers Park, where they'd turned in their kayaks, until all the boys had been picked up by their foster parents or birth parents, whatever the case might currently be.

Knowing he'd be there a while, he'd expected Riley to leave soon after they'd unloaded from the old bus that had driven them back to their drop-off spot. But rather than rush off, she'd stuck around, talking to the boys and their parents as Justin and the guide unloaded the bus.

Kyle still stuck close to her and Daisy, showing the dog to his foster family and telling them about how Daisy had loved sitting on the bow of the kayak and how she liked him so much.

Justin wasn't surprised when the boy threw his arms around Riley's waist and hugged her goodbye. Nor was he surprised when she hugged him right back in a hug full of emotion that was easy for anyone to see.

Easy for him to feel because it hit him right in the gut.

Riley might not have spent much time around kids, but she was good with them, full of compassion and patience.

He liked that about her.

He liked a lot of things about her.

But then, he already knew that.

She'd liked the boys, too.

Ashley had never connected with them, never bonded with them. No matter how much Justin had tried to involve Ashley in this special part of his life she'd resisted, claiming to be too busy with her residency, and then with work.

It hadn't been until the end that Justin had understood why.

His little charity, she'd called it.

Maybe because he'd been adopted, and viewed "family" as not just being bound by blood, he felt things she never had. Either way, the boys were so much more than his "little charity," and having them in his life had been a deal-breaker. He knew firsthand what a group like his could make in a foster child's life.

Ashley hadn't understood that.

Riley did. After just one day with the boys she got it.

Justin had wanted to wrap his arms around her and spin her around in glee when she'd said she wanted to bring them all home with her. That was exactly how he felt. What he'd do, given the chance.

Which might be happening soon with Kyle, depending on what his birth mother decided. *Would she let Kyle be adopted?*

After he'd been loaded into his foster family's vehicle, Riley came over to where Justin was strapping his kayak to the top of his Jeep. She'd changed out of her wet clothes into dry shorts and a T-shirt. They were a little tight, and accented her lush curves in ways that heated him more than the South Carolina sun.

She leaned against the side of the Jeep and smiled up at him. Good grief, she did a number on his insides. He'd kissed her, made love to her, and he wanted to do all that and more again. And she was smiling at him as if she was happy to be here with him.

Did he dare hope he'd finally gotten through to her that she was special?

"I think I'm in love."

As he battled suddenly weak knees, Justin's ears roared at her claim. Insides quaking, he grabbed hold of the Jeep to steady himself. Not that he thought she was talking about *him*. He knew she wasn't. But her words had twisted his insides around, playing havoc with logic.

"I can't imagine Kyle's foster family not wanting to keep him," she clarified. "I just met him and I adore him."

Kyle. Of course she meant Kyle.

"They've been taking kids in for years."

But he knew they had no plans to keep Kyle. He'd had multiple discussions with them when news of Kyle's mother's intentions had been made known.

"For some, that's what they want to do. Give kids a safe place to go for a few weeks or months." Thank God people like them existed, to give love and care so freely. "But many of the foster families don't feel equipped to take on one kid or more forever."

Thank God the Brothers family had. He and his siblings had gotten the cream of the crop when they'd been made official family members.

When he adopted—whether it was Kyle, one of the other Wilderness Group boys, or a child he'd yet to meet—Justin wanted to give that same cream-of-the-crop family experience.

Riley leaned against his Jeep and sighed. "I guess that makes sense…but I don't know how you could take a child in and then just let them go."

He understood. Because it was something he'd battled with since becoming involved with the boys. Having spent so much time with them, it was only logical that he'd want to adopt one of them, should that become a possibility.

"Don't think harshly of them. It's what they signed on to do. Foster parents do a great service, taking in kids who have nowhere else to go until the state figures out what's best for them."

"You're right. I know you're right. But still…" Her lower lip disappeared into her mouth.

He watched her closely. "You couldn't do it?"

"Be a foster parent?" She shook her head, looking down at Daisy in her arms and scratching the dog's neck. "I don't know… I'm not that great with kids but today, being with them— well, I can't imagine turning my back on them."

Justin's insides shook at her confession. Was that why he'd felt such urgency for her to come with them today? To see how she interacted with the boys? To see how they interacted with her?

Stan's wife had canceled on them, but they'd have been fine even if Riley hadn't gone with them.

He hadn't consciously been doing so, but if he'd been testing Riley she'd just aced the test.

And if she hadn't—then what?

Then nothing.

He'd never meant to become involved with anyone who didn't want a houseful of kids. Whether or not Riley wanted kids hadn't mattered. He'd been drawn to her and any "rules" he'd given himself about future romantic interests had been irrelevant.

"They'd be lucky to have you," he said, and meant it.

Her cheeks flushed a bright pink. "Ha! I know nothing about kids."

She looked so flustered it piqued his curiosity. "No natural instincts?"

"None."

He didn't believe her—not after having seen her with the boys. She'd opened right up to Kyle, had shown patience and kindness to the boy.

"I was an only child of an only child, so no siblings or cousins. And none of my close friends have kids," she continued. "If I do have natural maternal instincts they've not had any reason to come out."

"Until today?"

Her gaze lifted, and even though he couldn't see behind her mirrored glasses he knew her eyes were filled with surprise.

"You think I was being maternal today?"

Her question was raw—as if his answer mattered way more than it should, as if her merit was somehow being weighed. As it had at the party, her vulnerability shocked him.

"I think the boys, and Kyle in particular, brought out your protective instincts."

Considering what he'd said, and seeming pleased with the conclusions she drew, she smiled. "Maybe you're right."

"Haven't you figured it out yet?"

"What's that?"

"I'm *always* right," he teased, thinking that when it came to Riley he really had been. Right to think there was something special between them.

He might not be able to see behind her glasses, but he knew she was rolling her eyes, which didn't bother him in the slightest. She was smiling and so was he.

He glanced around the parking area. All the

kids except Stephen and Jevon were gone. The boys were sitting on the lowered tailgate of Stan's truck while Stan dug through a bag on the passenger floorboard.

Justin hesitated. As much as he wanted to suggest dinner, or whatever Riley would agree to, he couldn't just leave Stan with Jevon.

"I can stay with Jevon until he's picked up," he told Stan. Or until he drove him home, which was sometimes the case when the boy was at his birth mom's. She'd forgotten to come get him for one reason or another more than once. "If you need to get Stephen home?"

Stan shook his head. "I got this. You go ahead." He gestured toward Riley. "Nice to meet any friend of the doc's."

"Same," she agreed, holding Daisy close as she took one last look at Stephen's bandaged leg. "Take care of that knee so you're all well by our next adventure."

The boy nodded and Riley told him and Jevon goodbye. As she and Justin made their way to where she'd parked she was quiet.

"Thinking about all that yard work?" Justin teased. "There's still a lot of daylight left. I could help you knock it out this evening."

Ignoring his offer, she let Daisy jump into the

driver's seat, then turned back to him. "Thanks again for inviting me today. I wasn't sure about coming, but I'm glad I did for a lot of different reasons. Today's one of those days I'll think back on and always be grateful I experienced."

Despite the multiple layers of sunscreen applied at various points throughout the day her nose boasted a rosy pink color, as did her cheeks. He couldn't resist brushing his finger across her face.

"You're serious about coming with us again?"

She didn't pull away from his touch, or remind him he had no right to touch her. He supposed he didn't, but when she stared up at him, lips parted, looking hesitant, as if she wanted all the same things he wanted, he kept forgetting.

She nodded. "I'm looking forward to it."

"So am I."

He didn't want her to get into her car and drive away. He knew it was going to happen, and that the fact she'd spent the day with him at all was nothing short of a miracle. But he wasn't ready for it to end.

"Anything I can say that would convince you to spend the rest of the day with me?"

She inhaled deeply and he wished he could see what was in her eyes.

"I had a really great time…" she began.

"Does that mean you're considering having a really great rest of the day?" At her hesitation, he added, "As friends. Nothing more, if that's not what you want. You planned to do yard work. Let me help you."

"But…but that means inviting you to my house."

Hearing the possibility that she was going to say yes in her voice, he grinned. "I'd have trouble helping you with your yard work without being in your actual yard."

"Why would you want to do yard work with me?"

Unable to stand not being able to look into her eyes a moment longer, he lifted her sunglasses from her face, stared straight into her beautiful green eyes and told the truth.

"I'm not sure you get what I've been trying to convey to you for months."

Her eyes not leaving his, Riley swallowed.

"I like you," he admitted. "I want to date you. Not just take you to bed, like I think you assumed after Paul and Cheyenne's party, but to take you to dinner, help you with your yard work, spend time with you in ways that have nothing to do with sex."

Her eyes widened.

"I don't care who knows," he continued. "For that matter, I'd like there to be something for everyone to know."

Her lower lip disappeared into her mouth again as she stared up at him. "You're serious?"

He nodded. "Very."

Her long lashes swooped down over her cheeks and she kept her eyes closed for a few seconds, then lifted them and met his gaze. "I'm not sure this is smart, but would tomorrow be okay?"

Joy filled him. "Okay for you to be my girl-friend?"

Her eyes narrowed, but no walls went up. *Hallelujah.*

"Okay to help me with my yard work," she clarified, sounding very much like the in-charge nurse he was used to seeing. "Lucky you."

Although she was teasing, he *felt* lucky.

"The other thing is debatable," she said, her eyes darkening.

He felt her pulling away. He'd thought… No matter. She was letting him go over the following day. For now, that would have to be enough. No need to warn her that he'd been on his high school's debate team and they'd always won.

She'd know soon enough that he wouldn't give up easily.

"I'll take what I can get if it means getting to spend time with you."

With that, he leaned down and kissed her forehead. Her skin was warm beneath his lips. The touch was brief, but it felt right.

Just as Riley felt right.

"Special delivery."

Riley frowned through the peephole of her front door.

What had she been thinking, inviting him over? All night she'd tossed and turned, knowing that she had opened Pandora's box, was risking letting him in, risking the pain he could dole out.

Although she'd not recognized it at the time, she now knew Johnny hadn't been nearly the man Justin was. If Johnny's betrayal had gutted her so, how much more so would Justin's?

She'd considered canceling all morning, picking up her phone, typing out a message, deleting it, only to do the same thing again fifteen minutes later.

She opened the door and gestured to what he held. "What's that?"

He glanced down at the pizza box as if it had morphed into something unrecognizable. Arching his brow, he gave a sheepish grin. "Lunch?"

"I've already eaten."

Her cup of yogurt that morning had to count, because she didn't have the heart to tell him pizza was not on her diet. But the aromas were delicious and tempted her almost as much as he did.

"It's pizza. It'll keep until you work up an appetite." His gaze met hers as he added, "Doing yard work."

"Of course." She moved back for him to come inside, hoping she hadn't made a big mistake. Knowing she had.

"Not that I agree that you need to be dieting, but I did order cauliflower crust, in case you were still doing that low-carb thing."

Stunned, Riley stared at him. He'd ordered a low-carb pizza?

"Why?"

"Because I didn't want you to have a reason to say no."

To him or the pizza?

"You make it impossible to say no," she admitted, pointing toward her kitchen. "Just set the box on the counter." Because she sure couldn't take it from him. Not with the way her hands were shaking.

Although Johnny had constantly pointed out her jiggly thighs, he'd certainly never put any of her dietary needs before his. Quite the opposite. He'd order her favorites and then taunt her as he ate them.

Why, oh, why had she said yes to marrying him? Had she really been that desperate for love?

Justin set the pizza down, then turned to face her. "That's the idea, you know."

Trying to clear her head of the past, wondering if she should be desperately clinging to it instead, she blinked at the man now leaning against her countertop. He looked more scrumptious than anything she'd ever seen in her kitchen. Her mouth practically watered as she eyed him in his shorts, a T-shirt missing its sleeves, and tennis shoes.

"Making it impossible for me to say no?"

He nodded.

"I'm realizing that."

He grinned. "Maybe we could eat a slice or two before starting on the yard?"

She nodded. It wasn't as if she was going to

tell him he had to work on an empty stomach, particularly as he'd brought food.

Riley pulled a couple of plates from the cabinet. "Can I pour you a glass of water?" she asked.

"That would be great. You mind putting it into something that would be okay to take outdoors?"

She filled two reusable plastic water bottles, then handed him one. He'd already opened the box of pizza and removed a slice. Heaven smacked her nostrils.

"That smells so good."

He took a bite. "Tastes that way, too."

She eyed the pizza. "It would be rude for me not to have a slice."

His eyes twinkled. "It would."

"But just one..."

Justin wiped the sweat from his brow to keep it from running into his eyes, glancing around at their progress thus far.

He liked Riley's house—and her yard. The blue house had been built in the eighteen-hundreds and renovated several times over the decades since. The front yard boasted large rhododendrons, roses, azaleas and other flowering bushes Justin couldn't name but knew that his mother would have a fit over. And in the back Riley had a private oasis of sorts, with a large eucalyptus tree draped in tiny lights that he imagined must look magical at night.

That she had those whimsical lights said a lot about what she hid beneath her no-nonsense self-protective layers. There was a fire pit, a bench, several chairs, and off toward the back of the yard in a shady area was an over-sized hammock, hung between two large oaks.

Riley spent a lot of time in her yard and it showed.

The house itself was well taken care of, too, with high ceilings and glass vents above the doors giving testament to its age. Hardwood floors covered with the occasional colorful rug ran through the whole three-bedroom house. At some point someone had converted the back porch into a small washroom, and a new bathroom was now connected to Riley's bedroom.

Cassie rented the second bedroom, and the third seemed to be a catch-all with an exercise elliptical, a few ten-pound free weights, a shelf filled with books—mostly from nursing school—and a computer desk. The walls were decorated with colorful matching flower paintings signed by Riley and Cassie.

Yeah, he liked Riley's house, inside and out. Just as he liked *her*, inside and out.

"Cassie's with Sam," she'd told him earlier, while they'd been eating pizza.

She'd eaten two slices, all the while talking about how good it was, making him glad he'd gone to the trouble to search out low-carb pizza options prior to ordering.

His gaze ran over where she knelt now, pulling weeds from a flowerbed. She didn't need to diet, but if she thought so he'd do his part not to sabotage her. But he'd also do his part to make sure she understood that he liked her curves just as they were.

Perhaps sensing that he was watching her, she turned, glanced up at him, and smiled. His muscles clenched with memories, with elaborate longings. Not that he could act on them, no matter how she looked at him or tempted him. He'd promised himself he'd keep his hands off.

For today, at any rate.

So far they'd worked in her front yard and were making good progress. She'd purchased some mulch that she'd had stacked up next to a screened-in side porch. After weeding her landscaping, they'd spread the mulch around the knock-out roses and bushes in the front of her house.

"You want something to drink?" she asked.

"If you want to fill my water bottle up, that would be great." He'd almost finished what she'd put in there earlier.

She picked up the bottle and carried it inside, coming back out moments later. She handed it to him and surveyed their work. "I like it," she admitted.

"Me?"

"My landscaping," she corrected, giving him a teasing look. "Thanks for helping. Your strong back has made mincemeat of getting this done."

"I'm glad you let me help."

"Me, too." Taking a drink from her water bottle, she motioned to the remaining bag of mulch. "There's only the one left. I think we'll dump it in this side bed, and I'll mulch what's left of the back beds some other time."

"Just let me know when and I'll help."

Rather than agree, she looked away, and seemed unsettled by his offer.

Fighting a sigh, because for every two steps forward she felt it necessary to take one back, he picked up the bag of mulch, tore the plastic open, and began sprinkling the mixture over the flowerbed she'd indicated.

While he did so Riley trimmed a bush, dropping the cut pieces into a previously emptied mulch bag.

A few minutes later, live music filled the air. "Your neighbors are throwing a party?" he asked.

She shook her head. "There's a bandshell not far from here, in a small park. Local groups play there most weekends. Some are really good."

"So you lie in that hammock and listen to your own private concert?"

"Sometimes."

Her face said he'd hit on exactly what she often did. He'd thought as much. From the moment he'd stepped into her backyard he'd felt her presence, felt her connection to the retreat she'd created there.

"Is that where you were when we were texting the other night?"

She nodded. "I like being out there. Whether it's the eucalyptus or just being outdoors, my backyard soothes me."

"Now I understand why I couldn't tempt you to my place. Your backyard is amazing."

She beamed with pride. "It's not big or fancy, but it's home."

And it was an extension of her. Strong, beautiful, yet promising a fantasy escape from reality.

"How long have you lived here?"

"A coworker and her husband owned it. I'd visited a few times they had get-togethers and always felt a connection here. I'd just gotten engaged when it went up for sale. Thinking it would be our first home, I put a big chunk of my savings into a down payment. Obviously, as I'm not married, the engagement didn't work out…"

Had her voice broken a little just then?

"But I've no regrets on the house."

She'd been engaged.

Justin had known she'd had a bad break-up, but no one had mentioned that she'd actually been engaged.

"I didn't know you'd been engaged," he said.

"Failed relationships aren't exactly a priority conversation topic." She sighed. "My break-up was rather traumatic," she admitted.

Which made him wonder even more about the man she'd been engaged to but ultimately hadn't married.

"But that relationship did make clear several truths—one of which you should probably know, as it seems I'm having trouble staying away from you and you seem set on our dating."

She was considering dating him.

"I don't plan to marry."

Which sounded as if she'd been the one to call off her engagement. What had the guy done? Or had Riley just realized she was making a mistake? Just as he'd realized when he'd called off his own wedding?

"A couple doesn't have to marry to have a committed relationship."

"True." Her face pinkened. "And I don't mean to imply that you're even thinking in those terms. But, since you say you want to date me, it's only right to tell you that we wouldn't be headed in that direction. I'm not a get-married-and-have-kids kind of girl."

Justin *did* want a committed relationship with Riley. Maybe he'd want marriage to her someday, too. But the fact that she didn't want marriage wasn't a game-changer at this point in their relationship.

"What do you mean about kids?"

"I don't plan to have children."

"That's a shame."

"Because?"

"Because you were wonderful with the boys."

"I… Thank you. But that doesn't mean I should procreate."

"Procreating can be fun." He waggled his brows, trying to lighten the conversation, trying not to let his mind fall into a dark place where Riley was saying she didn't want kids. "Besides, there are other ways to have kids besides procreation."

"Such as volunteering with your Wilderness Group," she agreed. "Bringing more children into the world doesn't make sense when there are so many who need love."

Which Justin sort of agreed with.

"It feels weird to even be saying these things to you, but I just thought you should know how I felt—that, regardless of what happens between us, either of us can walk away at any time."

Since she was adamant that she didn't want the same things he did, perhaps Justin should walk away now. Not that he believed he could.

"Okay," he said slowly, trying to process the full implications of what she was saying. "I appreciate you telling me how you feel."

Too bad Ashley hadn't, or they'd never have gotten so close to walking down the aisle. At least with Riley he knew upfront that she could never be the one.

* * *

Unable to resist, Riley tore off the corner of a pizza slice from the box she'd stored in her fridge earlier.

Mmm. That was amazing, even cold.

Justin had made an effort to get her what he'd thought would make her happy. Because he wanted her happy. Which seemed unbelievable, really.

Just as the fact that he was in her shower right now was unbelievable.

Had someone tried to convince her earlier that week that he'd be in her bathroom, naked, with her water sluicing over his buff body, she'd have laughed.

Justin was in her bathroom naked!

Chewing her pizza, Riley leaned forward and pressed her head against the refrigerator. What was she doing?

You're having a great day, her inner voice reminded her. *A wonderful day with a wonderful man who brought you low-carb pizza.*

That alone should buy him major brownie points. That and all the other thoughtful things he did. For her and others.

But she shouldn't have him here—shouldn't

be wondering what he'd say if she walked into her bedroom and got into the shower with him?

"What am I doing?" she asked out loud, causing Daisy to look up from where she waited in hopes that Riley would drop some pizza crumbs.

"You talking to Daisy?"

Popping the last bit of pizza into her mouth, Riley spun. "Cassie! You're home!"

Surprised at Riley's odd reaction, her roommate gave a knowing smile. "Any reason I shouldn't be?"

"What? No, of course you shouldn't be. I mean, yes, you should be." Goodness, she was flustered. "I'm just surprised Daisy didn't bark when you came in."

Reaching down to pet the dog, Cassie grinned. "You're looking a little rattled. That have anything to do with the Jeep out front?"

Riley's face heated. "Oh, that."

"Yep, that." Cassie looked around the kitchen, even though it was obvious they were the only two there. "Where is he?"

"Who?"

"You know who. The owner of the Jeep. It's not as if I don't know who drives it."

On cue, the shower cut off and Justin began singing from her bathroom.

Cassie's eyes widened. "Oh, my. He's in your *shower*?"

"It's no big deal," Riley assured her.

"Right. Dr. Brothers is singing in your bathroom. No big deal."

"Okay, so it is a big deal. Sort of. But really, he's just there because he helped me with the yard. Besides, who else would it have been?"

Cassie walked over to the fridge, eyed the pizza box, raised a brow in surprise, then pulled out a cheese stick and peeled away the plastic. "The yard looks great."

"Yes, he was a lot of help."

"I bet he was." She took a bite of cheese.

"Cassie!"

Her friend laughed. "Sorry. Should I make myself scarce? If so, I can hang at Sam's tonight."

Riley shook her head. "It's not like that."

"The man is singing in your bathroom and you're blushing." Her roommate pointed her cheese stick at Riley. "Don't tell me it's 'not like that.'"

"Okay," Riley admitted, to herself and to Cassie, "so maybe it *is* like that..."

CHAPTER EIGHT

COMING OUT OF the bathroom, Justin walked into Riley's kitchen. "Nothing like that fresh from the shower feel," he said.

"Oh!" She jumped as he spoke, then frowned down to where Daisy sat at her feet. "That's twice in less than an hour you didn't bark. You're fired."

"Someone came by while I was in the shower?" He raked his fingers through his still damp towel-dried hair.

"Cassie came to grab some things on her way to Sam's."

"They're pretty serious?"

Riley laughed. "Depends what day you ask."

"Like that, is it?"

"Oh, yeah." She started pulling things out to prepare a meal.

"What are you doing?" he asked.

"Making us something to eat…"

He eyed the lettuce, cucumber, celery, and tomato. He wasn't opposed to salad, but he didn't foresee it filling him up. "I'd rather you go and do whatever you need to do and then we grab something."

She eyed him, then glanced back at what was on her countertop. "Not a salad kind of guy?"

"It's a nice first course," he admitted, watching her closely for any sign that his comment bothered her. That wasn't his goal. After working in her yard he'd need more than what was on her menu, though.

"Sorry." She gave a small smile. "I wasn't planning on company when I did my grocery shopping."

"No worries. We'll go somewhere—anywhere you like—and the next time you go grocery shopping you can plan for frequent company."

Her cheeks pinkened. "I could do that..."

"And I could be that company."

She laughed. "You think?"

"I hope."

Hesitating only a moment, she nodded. "Let me put this away, then give me a few minutes to get ready to go out."

She looked amazing to him already, but he knew she'd only blow off any compliment. "Sure, but I'll put this stuff away."

Her gaze lowered to the items, then she nodded. "Sounds good. Thanks."

Placing the items back into the fridge had only
taken Justin a minute, and while she showered
he wandered around Riley's house, looking at
the few knickknacks she had sitting around—
a few photos of her and Cassie, and a picture
of her and an older woman who must be her
mother.

She'd truly created a warm, comfortable home
and he was sitting in an overstuffed chair, Daisy
in his lap, when Riley came into the living room.

"You're beautiful."

She rolled her eyes. "You obviously got too
much sun today."

The fact that she refused to accept his compliments frustrated him. "If that were true it would
only explain this moment. What about every
other one since the moment we met?"

"Justin—"

"I'm serious, Riley. I find you beautiful. Don't
make light of it when I tell you so."

"I… Okay."

"I like how your shirt matches your eyes."

"I… Thank you."

"Good girl," he praised.

"Don't treat me as if I'm Daisy."

"I'm not. Daisy *expects* to be doted on. You're the exact opposite."

"You have a point," she agreed.

"For the record, I enjoy doting on you, Riley."

She sat down on the edge of a chair and motioned for Daisy to come to her. Daisy lifted her head, gave a look that said *Whatever*, then rested back against Justin.

"For the record, you've established that I'm the opposite of my very spoiled dog."

He laughed. "Maybe with time you'll let me spoil you."

"Don't hold your breath," she warned him.

For dinner, they ended up at a Mexican place, and discovered they had similar tastes in food.

"I don't eat out a lot, but I do love this yummy cheese sauce," she admitted, dipping a chip into the creamy mixture.

He could tell. Her face showed pure pleasure with every bite, and left him more interested in watching her than in eating. Not that that was anything new.

They talked about nursing school, med school, how they'd both arrived where they were in life now.

Justin couldn't recall a conversation he'd enjoyed more—not counting his talk with Riley at Paul and Cheyenne's party.

"I think they're going to throw us out of here if we don't leave soon," Riley mused.

Justin glanced around and realized they were the last customers in the restaurant, and that the staff were putting chairs up on empty tables.

"I guess more time has passed than I realized," he admitted, standing and dropping some money onto the table.

"Our waiter was giving us the evil eye the last time he asked if we wanted anything else," she teased. "There was still one other occupied table, so I didn't respond."

"I missed that." Because he had been too caught up in the woman sitting across the booth from him.

Between their kayak trip, the yard work, and their long dinner, he'd spent most of the weekend with her. An unexpected pleasure, for sure. But he still didn't want it to end.

When they pulled into Riley's driveway she didn't immediately get out of the Jeep, so neither did Justin.

Maybe she felt the same way he did.

"I—part of me wants to invite you in."

His heart pounded at her admission. He

wanted her to invite him in, but he also wanted her one hundred percent on board when that happened.

"I've mentioned how much I like that part of you. Still, I understand." He did. Mostly. "I'll walk you to the door, then leave."

She picked up her purse from the floorboard, as if she was going to get out, but still hesitated. "I…maybe we could sit in the backyard for a while?"

Pleased by her suggestion, Justin jumped on the offer. "I'd love to. If you're sure?"

"I'm sure." She got out of the car, headed to the back of the house, then paused. "I'll need to let Daisy out first, though."

"It's okay," he assured. "I promise I won't force my way into the house."

Her gaze cut to his. "That's not what I meant."

"I know. I'm teasing, Riley. I don't want you so nervous about my being here tonight. I was trying to lighten the mood."

"Sorry."

"I don't want you sorry, either."

Her gaze lowered, as if she carried a heavy emotional burden, but then she smiled—albeit an obviously forced one. "Today was wonderful, but it may take me a while to get used to the idea of you at my house."

Earlier, he'd wondered if she'd been the one to call off her engagement—now he asked himself what kind of a number her ex had done to her? He reached out to take her hand and gave it a gentle squeeze that he hoped conveyed she was safe with him. He'd never intentionally hurt her.

He hadn't intentionally hurt Ashley, either. But he *had* hurt her when he'd called off their wedding. She'd been floored that he'd chosen the boys over her.

He should have told Riley about his own past engagement earlier, when she'd mentioned hers. Something had held him back, though, telling him to wait until the time was right to mention that he'd come close to walking down the aisle, too, only to realize he was making a mistake.

He'd tell her about Ashley, but not now—not when Riley was just beginning to acknowledge what was happening between them.

Then again, she'd made it clear nothing long-term would be happening between them, so what did it matter if he told her about Ashley?

Riley admitted that Justin had been as good as his word. Not once had he made any attempt to go inside the house or tried to convince her to invite him in.

She'd let Daisy out into the backyard with them and the dog was now sleeping in her lap. She and Justin sat on the bench beneath the eucalyptus, talking, laughing, and she had to admit it was easy to forget to be nervous that they were alone when everything about the moment felt magical.

Or maybe that was just her fairy lights, casting a glowing spell.

She'd always found her backyard soothing. Tonight, next to Justin, with the night sky clear except for the dotting of twinkling stars, and the eucalyptus-laden breeze caressing her senses, she thought her backyard was the most romantic place on earth.

"Thank you for today, Justin."

He grinned. "Thank *you*."

"I'm serious. Today, and yesterday, too, were wonderful. It's been a really fantastic weekend. The best I can recall in a long time."

"And we still managed to get your yard work accomplished." He took her hand into his. "You should hang out with me more often."

In the glow of the fairy lights she stared at their entwined hands. How could something so simple cause millions of nerve cells to come to life? Cause her to want more of him touching her?

"Thanks for helping me with the yard."

Seeming oblivious to what his handholding was doing inside her, he said, "You have a great place."

"I think so."

Okay, this was crazy.

She gave a nervous laugh. "I'm making small talk."

"Why? We've been talking just fine."

Further torturing her, he lifted her hand to his lips and pressed a kiss there.

"I'm going to take this as my cue to leave and go," he said.

Her gaze hung on his.

Tell him to stay. Tell him not to go, to kiss you. All over.

She swallowed. "I think I'm ready for you to go home now."

He studied her a moment, then nodded. "Goodnight, Riley. I'll see you at the hospital tomorrow."

He gave her hand a gentle squeeze, then let himself out the back gate.

Riley sat outside on the bench for a long time

after Justin left and wondered exactly why she'd let him leave when they'd both wanted him to stay.

Wherein lay her answer.

Wanting him to stay wasn't what she needed to feel. Only she wasn't sure she could *not* feel that and so much more where Justin was involved.

She needed to be careful or she was going to end up hurt.

Riley wondered how Justin would be at the hospital the next time she saw him. Would he make a big deal over the fact they'd spent the weekend together or would he pretend it had never happened?

Good was her answer. He was good. Great, even.

Without saying anything untoward, he let her know with his smile, his wink, that he wanted to say more but would take his cue from her and wouldn't push it.

Even now, in the midst of repairing a torn medial meniscus, his gaze would connect with hers every so often, and in those brief moments she knew he was smiling beneath his surgical mask.

"Scalpel," he said, and the surgical assistant handed him the instrument.

The surgery went without any issues. And when they were finished Justin winked, then left the operating room.

The crew cleaned up the suite, then moved on to prepare for their next surgery—a knee being replaced by another orthopedic surgeon.

Two weeks passed, and with each day Riley found herself depending more and more upon the calls and texts she had from Justin.

And the time she spent with him.

Her brain kept screaming for her to put a halt to whatever was happening between them, but her lips could never sever their ties.

Tonight he'd invited her to the movies with the kids, showing up in a large SUV so they could go to pick up each boy.

Besides Stephen, six of the other boys planned to go. Four were currently with foster parents, including Kyle, and the two others were with their birth parents.

One birth mother seemed to have gotten her act together—was holding down a job and living with family members.

The other... Well, Riley knew she was going

to struggle to drop Jevon back at the junked-up little house where several other people besides he and his birth mother were living. It wouldn't be so bad, but two of the men living there had given Riley the creeps, and she was pretty sure they'd been carrying out a drug deal when Justin had pulled the van into a driveway crowded with vehicles.

Stan and his wife met them at the movie theater. Riley found her to be every bit as nice as her husband and liked her at once.

Justin bought hot dogs, popcorn, and drinks for everyone, and when they were settled into a row he and Riley sat at one end and Stan and his wife at the other, with all seven boys in the middle.

Riley leaned over and whispered, "You're a really nice guy, Justin Brothers."

"You only just now figuring that out?" He grinned.

"I'm a slow learner."

"I don't buy that—which means I'm not nearly as nice as you think."

"Probably not, but what you're doing for these boys is wonderful." Riley glanced at Kyle, who'd insisted upon sitting next to her, then back at Justin. "I hate that he's upset I didn't bring Daisy," she whispered. "I had to remind him multiple times that pets aren't allowed in the movie theater complex."

Justin chuckled. "I'll plan something soon that Daisy can attend."

"Or maybe I can bring Daisy to visit him." She frowned. "Is that allowed? For me to visit the boys?"

"It shouldn't be a problem. I can talk with his foster parents and set up something."

"I'd like that," she said, and meant it.

"They'll likely want me there, too, until they get to know you."

"Shh!" someone hissed from behind them.

Riley's face heated.

Justin laughed and gave an *uh-oh* look.

She turned back to the movie, intent on watching the space story and not being one of "those" people who talked all through a movie.

When Kyle reached over and grabbed her hand, lacing his smaller fingers with hers, Riley wanted to hug him for the sweet gesture.

When Justin took her other hand she smiled, but wasn't sure if she wanted to hug him too or pull her hand away. Not because she didn't want to hold his hand, but because of the heat zapping from his body to hers at the skin-to-skin contact.

Justin holding her hand made her heart pound. Her stomach twist. Made her want to hug him with nothing between their bodies. Made her very aware of how very domestic they appeared, with her in between Justin and Kyle.

She shouldn't be doing this. So why was she?

Grimacing at her thoughts, she stared at the movie screen but could no longer concentrate on the alien life forms trying to take over the earth.

An alien life form was trying to take *her* over.

Or it sure felt that way.

She cut her gaze to Justin.

Popping a piece of popcorn into his mouth with his free hand, he was watching the movie with great interest. As if his holding her hand was no big deal and was not affecting him in the slightest.

At least one of them was enjoying the film.

Then, without looking toward her, he squeezed her hand, letting her know he was aware of her watching him. Maybe he was even aware of what was happening inside her, because his hand held hers a little tighter.

After the movie, they dropped the kids off at their respective homes. Jevon was their last passenger, and Riley's stomach knotted more the closer they got to where they'd drop him off.

The boy had moved to the front row of seats in the SUV, preventing Riley from voicing her concerns about bringing him back home to Justin.

Fortunately, when they got to Jevon's, although there were still several cars in the driveway, there was no sight of the creepy men. Justin walked Jevon to the front door, keeping his hand on the boy's shoulder while he talked for a few minutes to a harried-looking pregnant woman, with a baby on her hip and another tugging at her shirt-hem.

Riley couldn't hear what was being said, but saw the woman nodding a lot, then hugging Justin after he handed her something. Money, most likely.

How could Riley not like a man who did such good? Sure, he'd break her heart if she let him, but the man was one of the kindest people she'd ever met.

When he pulled the SUV into her driveway Riley didn't hesitate, and nor did she question whether Justin would follow suit.

No one was at the house, so they let Daisy out into the backyard. Following the dog, Justin headed toward the bench where they'd spent hours beneath the eucalyptus tree and the fairy lights.

Riley hesitated, and then, heart pounding, asked, "Want to lie on the hammock with me for a while?"

"Absolutely. I've been waiting for you to invite me."

They'd spent several evenings in her backyard, but for whatever reason she hadn't asked him onto the hammock. Tonight she didn't turn on the fairy lights, opting for the twinkling stars and lying in the hammock. With Justin. Large tree limbs would partially block their view, but there would be plenty of sky shining through to gaze upon.

"You first," she told him when they reached the hammock, thinking it would be easier for her to get in if he was already there.

Justin climbed into the hammock, took Daisy from her, then patted the space beside him. "Your turn."

Being careful not to flip him out, Riley got into the hammock and snuggled next to him. She became instantly alert at the feeling of her body against his. Over the past couple of weeks he'd held her hand, kissed her hand, even her forehead, but he'd never kissed her lips or pressed his body to hers.

She wasn't sure why. Part of her appreciated it that he hadn't pushed. Another part—well, that other part was sorely disappointed and tonight seemed to be taking charge.

Although usually the eucalyptus filled her senses, Justin overpowered everything, with his long lean body, his spicy scent, his warmth…

"This is nice." He laced his hand with hers.

"It's one of my favorite places to be," she admitted, wondering if she meant in the hammock or his arms.

"In my arms?"

Had he read her mind? "In the hammock," she assured him, but wasn't positive she'd told the complete truth.

Which was a little scary.

A lot scary.

There was a light breeze that put the slightest chill in the air, making the warmth of his body next to hers more appealing, and she wrapped her arm around his waist, holding him tight, pretending she didn't notice the way his abs contracted beneath her fingers.

"Cold?"

Not really, but after moving nearer what could

she say? That she was trying to get closer even though their bodies were already pressed side by side?

"I can go inside and get that quilt you keep on the back of the sofa if you want me to," he offered.

"I'm fine," she assured him, her fingers tracing a pattern over his stomach.

"Tell me about that quilt. It looks old."

Did he really want to talk? Because *she* didn't.

"It is old. It was my mother's. Her grandmother made it for her."

"You've mentioned your mother before—that she gave you the necklace you lost. I've noticed the photo you have of the two of you in your living area. What about your dad?"

Now she *really* didn't want to talk.

"What about him?"

"What does he do? Where does he live? Why are there no photos of him?"

Riley fought the stiffening of her muscles and the urge to tell Justin to mind his own business. "I don't know, I don't know, and he left when I was four. Any photos that existed of him were gone long before I was old enough to know what they were."

"Sorry."

"Don't be. I had a great mother and a great childhood. She worked hard. We were poor. But we never went hungry or without love. I feel blessed. It could have been so much worse—like with the boys in your Wilderness Club."

"I'm glad your mom was able to take good care of you." He paused. "What happened to her?"

Riley didn't feel like talking about her mother or the past, but she answered him. "She passed in an automobile accident, not long after I graduated from university."

"I'm sorry, Riley. She sounds like she was a great lady."

"She was. She'd have liked you."

She'd have adored him. Kindhearted, smart, handsome—what more could a mother hope for, for her daughter?

"Oh? Tell me more."

"She liked handsome men who talked a good game."

He strained his neck the better to look at her. "You think I'm handsome?"

She rolled her eyes. "You know you are, Justin."

"How would I know that?"

"A mirror?"

He laughed. "I don't think much about the way I look."

"Beautiful people usually don't."

"I'd argue with that. Some of the most beautiful women I know obsess about how they look. They pick themselves apart, seeing flaws where none exist."

"A lot of not so beautiful people do that as well."

"We do tend to be our own worst critics. Usually because someone has torn down our belief in ourselves."

She considered his comment and couldn't argue. Hadn't she been a wreck after the end of her involvement with Johnny?

"For the record, you have no need to pick anything. You're perfect as you are," he said.

"You're saying that because you want to date me?" she ventured.

He shook his head. "Because I *am* dating you."

Justin felt Riley stiffen in his arms and wondered if he should have kept his thoughts to himself. They'd had such a great time, the last thing he wanted was to put her on guard.

"*Are* we dating?" Riley asked.

Choosing his words carefully, he took her hand into his. "Yes, Riley, we are dating."

She lay in his arms for a long time, not saying anything, just holding his hand and breathing softly as they swung in the hammock.

"I never meant for that to happen."

"I did."

She didn't look at him, just stared upward at the sky peeking through the tree limbs. "But you've barely touched me the past few weeks and you sure haven't tried to have sex with me."

Her words were a mix of breathiness and accusation. He hugged her closer to him, wanting to calm the demons that made her doubt herself. "Not because I haven't *wanted* to touch you or have sex with you. Believe me, I have."

"Do you think you'll still want to date me after we have sex again?"

The uncertainty in her voice had him turning onto his side to face her. "Do you think I won't? Because that's a pretty easy theory to disprove."

"By our having sex?"

"Obviously."

"Is that a proposition?"

"Is it working?"

"No."

"Then I need to try harder."

With that, Justin rolled so that his body covered hers. He supported his weight on his elbows and stared down at her, giving her a minute to tell him to get off her if that was what she wanted.

Instead, eyes wide, she smiled up at him. "I don't know how you did that without toppling us out of the hammock, but I'm impressed."

"You only just now figuring out I have skills?" he teased, waggling his brows and trying to remind himself to take things slow. Easier thought than done, with his body stretched out over Riley's.

Daisy jumped down from the hammock.

"Hmm…" Her gaze lowered to his mouth. "I don't think Daisy was nearly so impressed."

Fighting the urge to flex his hips more fully against her, Justin replied, "Daisy needs to learn who's boss."

Riley's gaze lingered on his mouth. She *had* to feel his reaction, *had* to know how she was affecting him.

"I suppose you think you're an expert at teaching females you're the boss?"

What he thought was that Riley was an expert at shooting his temperature through the roof.

"She's a good dog…just needs the right encouragement."

"What did you give my dog?"

He grinned down at her. "The right encouragement."

"You're good at that, aren't you?"

"Giving the right encouragement?" he asked, knowing they were no longer discussing her dog.

"Getting females to do what you want them to do."

Riley lay still beneath him on the hammock. Their bodies were pressed together and he was propped up on his elbows so he could see her face. Good thing, otherwise he'd have missed the swirling emotions in her eyes. Emotions that conveyed the way he affected her, making her want to draw nearer and back away at the same time. He'd been patient, given her space, but maybe she needed the right encouragement too.

"Maybe. Let's see," he told her, his voice low, husky.

His gaze went to her lips, then back to her beautiful eyes. He wanted her to kiss him. He waited, wondering if she'd hold out for him to make the first move, or perhaps push him away. She stared at him, clearly warring with the voices in her head, then seemed to come to a conclusion—a good conclusion.

She wrapped her arms around his neck to cradle his head and she arched up from the hammock to kiss him.

Her mouth was warm against his…soft. Sweet. Promising so much more than a quick peck. Making him want to forget patience and take control.

But he wouldn't.

Riley needed to do this—to be the one in control as her mouth explored his.

Her fingers curled into his hair, cradling him, holding him close as their kiss deepened.

When she lay back she stared up at him, with wide eyes and plump lips. He'd never seen anything more beautiful than the sight of her beneath him, staring up at him in awe.

"Thank you," he whispered, bending to kiss the tip of her nose. He let out a breath he hadn't realized he'd been holding, in the fear that she'd tell him to leave. "Thank you for kissing me, Riley."

"You're welcome."

Her gaze met his, darkened with what he could only describe as passion.

"Do you want me to kiss you again?" she asked.

Was that a trick question?

"More than anything," he said.

Riley kissed him again and again.

Justin was the best man Riley had ever known. In so many ways. Kind, patient, tender… Even now, when she could feel how tense his body was, how every sinew was strained tight, his lips were gentle against hers, as if she was fragile and must be handled with care.

Perhaps she was.

Not physically, but emotionally.

"What I'm about to do may not work, and you may not forgive me," he warned.

Before she could do much more than register what he'd said, much less wonder what he planned, Riley gasped as Justin rolled them so he was on the bottom and she lay across him.

"I've no idea how you did that without us falling out," she admitted, holding on to his shoulders as if she thought they might still topple.

"That was the part you might not have forgiven. If we'd ended up on the ground because of my miscalculation."

"You calculated well."

"Apparently," he agreed. "As I have you against me."

"It's where I want to be," she admitted, wrapping her arms around his neck.

"Riley…" he groaned, his body contracting beneath hers, his hips arching upward.

Pulling him so his lips hovered just above hers, she smiled. "You know those skills you mentioned earlier…?"

He nodded.

"You're going to need them."

His eyes widened. "You're sure?"

"Positive. I want you."

"No regrets?"

Regret was inevitable. Surely he knew that? She wanted peace and contentment in her life. Being with him was utter chaos. At least it felt that way to her nerves. Yet she couldn't stay away—much as a moth was drawn to a flame, knowing it was flying to its demise, but flapping its wings with all its might to go down in a blaze of glory.

"I want you," she repeated. "Now."

"Here?" he clarified, still seeming afraid to believe her and giving her plenty of time to change her mind if that was what she wanted.

It wasn't.

Going in for another kiss, then another, she whispered against his lips, "You have those skills, right? Show me..."

CHAPTER NINE

"I'M NOT SURE what I did to my knee," Cassie mused, carefully climbing onto Justin's examination table. "Sam and I were at a restaurant that had steps and my knee started to hurt. I didn't feel or hear any pop prior to the pain hitting."

Justin dried his just washed hands and turned to his patient, doing his best to focus on her and not on the woman who'd brought her to this appointment. The woman he was absolutely crazy about and had spent every spare moment with over the past few months.

There were times when he still felt those walls she refused to let go of, that he longed to knock down completely, and felt her clinging to them as a protective shield, but they'd come a long way from her sneaking out of his condo.

"How long ago was it that you first noticed a problem?" he asked, sitting down on his stool and rolling toward Cassie, where she was sitting on the examination table.

"A week ago."

A week ago he and Riley had sat on a blanket, watching a band make use of the bandshell at the park near her house.

Unable to avoid doing so a moment longer, he glanced toward where she sat. Their gazes collided and she smiled. His heart quivered like a fish out of water. Because that was what it did when Riley smiled at him a certain way.

The way that said she knew what he liked and she liked it, too.

The way that said she wanted him.

She *did* want him. For the past couple of months she'd not pretended otherwise. Most of the time. Although she kept herself emotionally guarded, physically she held little back.

Flashing her a quick smile, he dragged his gaze from hers and forced himself to focus on her roommate. "Any improvement since you felt the initial pain?" he asked.

Cassie shook her head. "The pain keeps getting worse. It's not too bad when I first get up in the morning. But the more I do, the worse it feels." She frowned. "It's interfering with my work, my everything. And I don't feel safe driving—which is why I had Riley bring me today."

At the mention of her name, his gaze went

back to the pretty woman sitting on the opposite side of the examination room. Sure, he knew she'd never let her guard down completely, but he was hopeful he would eventually earn her trust.

Which was an issue.

He'd still not told her about Ashley, and nor had she opened up about the details of her broken engagement. Talking about Ashley never felt appropriate while he was with Riley. Did she feel the same about her ex with him? Maybe they needed to forget their pasts, not worry about mistakes made before they'd even met.

Not that he bought that.

Nor could he shake the feeling that he was constantly trying to earn Riley's acceptance. Hadn't he learned as a child that you couldn't earn love? If so, his birth mother would have adored him.

"I've tried all the things we tell our patients to do, but not noticed much of a change," Cassie continued, oblivious to the fact that his attention had strayed.

Chiding himself, he forced his attention back on Cassie. Getting her to sit on the exam table with her legs hanging over the edge, he visually inspected both her knees, then grasped her right knee, placed his palm over her patella and, holding on to her ankle, put her leg through a passive range of motion. She had smooth movement, with no noises or reported pain, and he easily achieved greater than one-hundred-and-thirty-degree flexion.

He started to do the same to her left, but Cassie grimaced as he attempted to move her leg so he stopped. He'd only achieved about ninety degrees.

He quickly did varus and valgus tests, noting the difference in results, then palpated the patella, feeling along the tibial plateau for abnormalities. He checked for a fluid shift, noting she was positive for effusion on the left knee. He ran through anterior and posterior drawer tests, then an Apley test, checking the collateral ligaments and for meniscus tears.

Having her position herself so her legs swung freely off the table, he took a reflex hammer out of his scrub pocket and struck just below and slightly lateral to her patella. He didn't think she had any spinal issues, but wanted to make sure the deep tendon reflex was normal. They were symmetric, and within normal ranges bilaterally.

"Stand and walk across the room," he told her.

Grimacing, Cassie got off the table and hobbled toward the exam room door and back. Justin studied her gait, making note of how she distributed her weight.

"All your tests for tissue tears are negative, so it's likely just inflammation. I'd recommend pulling the fluid off, an injection, compression, ice and rest, followed by some physical therapy you can do at home or at a center—whichever you prefer."

Cassie nodded. "I'm willing to try anything."

Justin drew up the injection, pulled out a drape, antibacterial skin prep pads, gloves, and some anesthetic spray. He turned to Riley. "You okay with helping?"

Riley stood to wash her hands and put on a pair of gloves. She hadn't expected to participate in Cassie's treatment. But, since she'd asked Justin to see her today, she wasn't going to refuse.

"If you'll tell me what to do," she said.

With Cassie on the table, her leg slightly flexed, Justin pressed along the lateral condyle, looking for a good entry point. He marked his spot with the top of the needle cap, pressing just hard enough to indent the skin. Donning gloves, he cleaned the area with antiseptic preparation, then picked up the syringe.

"If you'll spray the anesthetic at the marked area, please?"

Riley aimed the anesthetic, spraying until the skin blanched, and Justin pushed the needle into the desensitized area.

Watching Justin in an office setting was a new experience. At the hospital they were usually in surgery together, with his patient asleep. His movements were just as efficient today as at any other time she'd seen him work. Something she'd had the opportunity to do in and out of the hospital almost daily these past few months.

Because she couldn't seem to stay away—had quit trying, for the most part. Every so often fear would remind her that she was playing with fire, that she was going to hurt both herself and Justin. Still, she couldn't stay away.

He injected a small amount of anesthetic, then switched the syringe over to an empty one. Re-checking the position, he pulled back on the plunger. The syringe filled with straw-colored fluid.

When he was ready, Riley handed the medication-filled syringe. Needle still in place inside the numbed area on Cassie's knee, he carefully exchanged the aspirated syringe with the medication one, handing the other to Riley. When he felt a pop, indicating the needle was where it should be, he injected the medication into the joint space.

"You okay?"

"Never better," Cassie said through gritted teeth.

"You're doing great," Riley praised her as Justin withdrew the needle.

Riley immediately covered the area with sterile gauze and applied pressure.

"Remember—compression, ice, and rest, then knee-strengthening exercises." He printed a home exercise sheet, and an order for formal physical therapy, and handed them to her. "I'm writing you a note. I don't want you on your feet much for the next couple of days. And you—" he turned to Riley "—I'll see tonight, when I bring dinner for all three of us."

"I *knew* I liked him," Cassie said.

"That makes two of us," Riley agreed, applying a bandage over her friend's knee.

Only eventually he'd tire of her and leave. Then what?

* * *

"Me, me! Please. I want to go next," Kyle called, bouncing and waving his hand as he waited his turn to have his photo taken in the oversized chair in front of the forty-foot-tall boy at the children's museum.

Riley smiled down at the excited boy who'd stuck so close to her most of the day. She loved these outings she took with the Wilderness Group, and had even taken Daisy to visit with Kyle a few times. His foster family was wonderful. She hoped they'd adopt Kyle if that ever became a possibility.

The Wilderness Group had done a big photo earlier, everyone included, and were now doing individual pictures. There were only two boys who hadn't been in front of the exhibit yet. And Stephen looked as if he couldn't care less as he and another boy discussed something they'd seen earlier in the day.

"Okay!" Justin laughed at the boy's exuberant request. "You're next. Need a hand climbing up?"

Kyle's forehead puckered. "I got this, Captain Brothers." Only rather than attempting to get in the chair, he turned to Riley. "Will you be in a picture with me?"

As in just the two of them? She looked to Justin for guidance and he shrugged, leaving it up to her.

"I think you're supposed to have an individual picture right now, but I'll be in a photo with you later, if you want."

Kyle nodded, as if he understood, but disappointment shone on his face.

Riley looked to Justin. As always, her heart sputtered—probably in disbelief that they were a couple and had been for several months. She barely believed it and yet she was living it.

She'd never thought she'd be in a relationship again. Had never thought she'd risk doing so. Was it possible she'd been wrong? That Justin was worth taking a chance on and wouldn't break her heart?

Part of her wanted to believe it was true. Another part warned her that she was being foolish and would deserve the heartache that would head her way if she fell for such nonsense.

"Smile," Justin told the little boy, who seemed to have gone from a bundle of energy to a flat tire.

Did having a photo taken with her mean that much to him? Goodness, but he was getting attached. She probably shouldn't encourage him, but she couldn't stand to see his disappointment.

Rather than try to get Justin's attention, Riley darted into the picture, spread her arms wide in a total photo-bombing pose near to where Kyle sat, and cried, "Cheeseburgers!"

Surprised, Kyle laughed, wrapped his arms around her neck from behind in a hug, and repeated, "Cheeseburgers!"

When she was sure Justin had gotten the shot, she turned and hugged Kyle. "Now, we better let him get a picture of just you, too, since he was nice enough to bring us here today."

Kyle nodded and gave a toothy grin.

Shaking his head, Justin chuckled, snapped the shot, then helped Kyle down. He took Stephen's photo next, then one of Stephen with Stan.

When he was done, he joined Riley where she waited and pulled up the photo-bomb picture. "Do you see his face? You made his day."

Kyle did look ecstatic at her silliness. For that matter, so did Justin.

"Good. He deserves lots of smiles."

"As do you."

Justin leaned in and planted a quick kiss on her mouth. Something he'd done a lot of the past couple of months. Lot of kisses. Lots of more than kisses.

"Not here in front of the kids," she scolded, but they both knew she didn't mind a light PDA.

Justin chuckled. "Afraid you won't be able to resist pulling me off to some private corner and having your way with me?"

"Have you looked around this place? It's crawling with kids—literally. There are no private corners. Now, are we going to see if this tall boy exhibit teaches us anything about human anatomy?"

"I'd rather hold out for a private lesson later."

Riley clicked her tongue. "Now, now, Dr. Brothers. What will the boys think if their leader doesn't forge their path?"

"That's he's lucky to be with you?"

She laughed. "Good answer—but let's go check out the exhibit with the kids."

"Wait, look at this first."

Riley glanced at his camera screen. After her photobombing he'd continued to snap photos, and had gotten one of Kyle hugging her. Gravity tugged at her insides at the sight of the emotion on his face, the freely given love.

"You know, for someone who once claimed

not to know anything about kids, you sure have let the boys grow on you."

She enjoyed the Wilderness Group, and was grateful to be a part of the boys' lives. They'd enriched her life—especially Kyle, who always sought her out and made her feel special.

"They're awesome kids," she said.

But perhaps she needed to pull back, not encourage Kyle so much. She didn't want him to get too attached to her. The last thing she'd ever want would be to hurt him.

"Agreed—and you're awesome with them."

Justin's compliment made her insides gooey. She did enjoy the boys, but it wasn't as if she was doing anything more than spending a few hours here and there with them.

They headed around to the entrance to the tall boy exhibit, where the kids could explore the human body structure inside of it.

"You'd make a great mother, Riley."

Justin's words struck deep, bringing old insecurities to the surface, and the words Johnny had tossed at her in the aftermath of their failed wedding.

Why would he marry an overweight woman like her? He wouldn't want to risk his kids taking after her. He wouldn't—

Riley stopped her thoughts, knowing her insecurities would choke her out if she let them. She wouldn't let them.

And, although his sentiments were so different from Johnny's, Justin's words cut into her, making her feel the need to set the story straight.

She stopped walking, turned to Justin, and shook her head. "No, I wouldn't."

He stared at her as if he didn't know what to say. He probably didn't.

"I won't have children," she reiterated, wanting to make sure he understood.

It was something she'd decided after Johnny had left her at the altar. She'd go through this life alone, because it was easier with no one to leave her again.

Only she was so involved with Justin, she wasn't really going it alone, was she?

Panic gurgled up her throat.

Justin's forehead scrunched, then his expression softened with compassion. "Sorry, I know you said— I just thought—"

He thought she'd changed her mind because she'd been hanging out with him and the boys. Did he not realize how she felt? How having a child would only set her up for pain? Why would she want children when everyone she loved left?

She'd been foolish to let Justin get so close, because sooner or later he'd do the same.

Justin's blood cooled. He shouldn't have pushed with that comment about Riley making a good mother. He'd known better. So, why had he?

She didn't want children.

Listening to her make her claim had brought back memories of Ashley. Which wasn't completely fair. Ashley hadn't been opposed to children of her own, just not fostered or adopted.

Riley didn't want either.

Even after spending the past few months with him and the boys her feelings hadn't changed. Would they ever?

He'd been so into Riley that he'd continued to pursue their relationship even after she'd told him she didn't want children. He had no right to be upset now, at hearing her repeat what she'd said all along.

Only he was.

How could she spend time with him and Kyle and not want more? Not want to be a part of their forever?

"I'm sorry," he backtracked, knowing his

comment had triggered what he usually did his best to avoid: Riley's walls. "I didn't mean to upset you. It's just that you're wonderful with the boys...with Kyle."

"I adore them, but that doesn't mean I want children of my own," she clarified, not meeting his eyes. "I told you from the beginning that I didn't."

"I know you did, but—"

She took a step back, causing him to realize that he'd sharpened his tone. Something he rarely did with anyone, and that he sure didn't want to do with her or the boys. He took a deep breath, then raked his fingers through his hair.

"But you thought I'd change my mind?" she asked.

"I've heard you say more than once that you want to take the boys home and keep them," he reminded her, fighting to keep the accusation out of his voice.

Riley didn't respond, just stared at him, shock and uncertainty shining in the green depths of her eyes.

What was wrong with him? he asked himself. He knew better than to push. He never pushed. Because so long as he didn't she wouldn't build new walls between them.

Right now, new walls were going up.

"I… Maybe we should talk about this later?" she suggested, not quite meeting his eyes.

She was right. They were at the children's museum with the Wilderness Group, and they had been having a good time. A great time. Now wasn't the place to have this conversation.

His phone buzzed in his pocket and, grateful for the reprieve, he glanced at his smart watch to see who the message was from.

His lawyer.

It was a Saturday. If Mary was texting there must be news on Kyle's mother.

Heart thundering, Justin swallowed the lump that had formed in his throat. Would today be the day his life changed forever? If it did, what was Riley going to think about that change?

She knew how he felt about the boys, but he'd never told her he planned to adopt Kyle. She'd already said she didn't want marriage and children. He could live without marriage so long as they were committed to each other. But no children…

His heart ached at the thought.

No children wasn't a possibility for him. His whole life he'd planned to have kids—to adopt, to foster. Soon, hopefully, he'd be a father.

It was something that scared him, but it was a challenge he'd gladly face. He had a lot to learn, but if Kyle's mother signed the papers and the courts granted him custody Justin would do right by the kid. He'd love him and raise him to the best of his abilities. Just as his parents had adopted, loved, and raised him.

Which meant putting Kyle first—above his own needs.

But where did that leave his relationship with Riley? She didn't want children, but did that mean she wouldn't want *him* to have them either?

If not, did that mean it was time to let go?

If so, how exactly did he do that, when letting go was the last thing he wanted?

CHAPTER TEN

"WHAT ARE MY odds of success?"

Justin clenched his cellphone in his sweaty hand, waiting anxiously for his lawyer's response. He'd snuck away from the group as soon as he could to call Mary back.

On her way to prison, Kyle's mother had signed away her rights rather than leave the boy dangling in court custody indefinitely. Kyle was adoptable. Mary had already drawn up the papers and had them ready to go, so they could move quickly to make Kyle his.

Justin had always planned to adopt one of the Wilderness Group, to make one of the boys his permanently. Kyle had always reached out to him more than the others, had always seemed a bit different. That he would be Justin's seemed like fate.

"You have a great shot. Not as good as if you were married and bringing a two-parent household to the table," his lawyer warned him. "But as you've been involved in Kyle's life for several years and are financially solvent, and you have letters of recommendation from Kyle's current foster parents, and you're an upstanding member of society, the judge should grant your petition."

"When will we know something for sure?"

"Kyle's mother just signed the papers yesterday. These things don't always move quickly."

After as long as he'd been involved with the boys, Justin knew she was right—but he wanted answers. Wanted to know whether or not to tell Riley that Kyle's mother had signed her rights away and he planned to adopt him.

She'd told him she didn't want kids. If he adopted Kyle did that mean she'd not want to continue their relationship?

But she adored Kyle. He couldn't imagine her walking away. He didn't want to imagine her doing so.

"I'll call when I know more, but I thought you'd want to know she signed the papers and I filed your petition late yesterday afternoon. I didn't have a chance to update you then. We'll have more answers soon."

"Thanks."

"Good luck, Justin. I know how much this means to you."

Yeah, adopting had been his goal even before becoming an orthopedic surgeon had.

Justin hung up the phone, thought about pulling Riley aside now, because he'd really like to tell her everything, to share all the things he was feeling, all the *what ifs*, but thought better of it.

Maybe he would have, had they not just had the discussion they'd had, but not now. He was going to have a difficult enough time pretending that everything was fine for the rest of the afternoon without Riley also pretending. Not that he didn't want to shout to the world that Kyle might be his soon, but he didn't want to get Kyle's hopes up in case the judge decided against him.

If the adoption went through, his life would undergo major changes. Changes such as him needing to find a house with a yard for Kyle to play in, needing to make sure that wherever he moved was zoned for a good school system, making sure that when he signed on to be the boy's father he took that commitment seriously and put Kyle first.

Yeah, between Riley's declaration and his lawyer's call, Justin's focus would be shot for the rest of the afternoon. Good thing all they had left to do was the Flight Adventure and simulator. After that, the boys should all have rides home and he'd go and run to clear his head—because everything was a jumbled-up mess.

Or maybe it was just where Riley was concerned that he'd made a mess of things…by wanting what she'd said from the beginning that she didn't.

Riley pasted on a smile when Justin rejoined their group. They'd been having such a lovely time that she hated how things had gone downhill—hated even more how nervous she felt when she glanced toward him now.

"Sorry," he murmured, getting in line beside her as a museum worker talked to the group about aviation, then let each boy take a turn pretending to fly a plane in the cockpit that had been built into the side of the building, to give the kids a lookout over Columbia during their "flight."

Riley had never been in a plane. She'd never had reason to, so she was as fascinated as the boys. Or would have been had she been able to keep her eyes off Justin.

He'd pulled his phone out again, checking to see if he had any new messages.

"Everything okay?" she asked.

He turned toward her but didn't meet her eyes. "Fine."

"Was that the hospital earlier?"

"The hospital?"

Whoever it had been, the call had had his eyes darkening.

"No. Why?"

"You seem distracted. I wondered if something was up with a patient."

"No. Everything's fine as far as I know."

"Good."

Only, everything was not fine, because he'd gone from lots of PDA to barely acknowledging that she existed.

Then again, it might not have anything to do with the text and everything to do with the conversation they'd been having.

Justin was great with kids—obviously he wanted children. At some point he'd have to move on in order to have those things. Maybe it wasn't fair of her to hang onto their relationship knowing she didn't want them.

Why had she given in to her desire to spend time with him? Let him become a part of her daily life to the point where she couldn't imagine a single day without him in it?

Her heart hurt at the thought that soon she wouldn't need to imagine it. Because Justin was going to leave.And soon.

She felt it with every bit of her being.

Felt it and needed to brace herself for it.

He was tense the rest of the afternoon. He had been since his off-the-wall comment, but whoever had texted him had totally pulled him out of the game. And not just with her, but the boys, too.

He said all the right things, smiled at all the right times, but his eyes were far away, as was his mind.

At last, Riley hugged the boys goodbye, got into Justin's Jeep, and was grateful the wind made it difficult to talk, because that at least gave them a reason for silence.

When he pulled into her driveway she turned to him, searching for something to say that would erase whatever had changed between them.

"Thanks for going with us today," he said.

At least he was talking to her. "You're welcome. Thanks for inviting me."

Ugh. They sounded awkward—like two strangers forced into each other's proximity.

"Did you bring clothes to change into for our run?" she asked.

They'd planned to go to the park and get in a few miles, then head back to her place to clean up and go to dinner.

Justin grimaced, then shook his head. "Something's come up. I'm going to take a rain check on our run and our dinner plans."

He was canceling their plans.

Justin was canceling their plans.

And just like that she knew the end had started.

She nodded as if she understood, and reached for the door handle. She did understand.

She didn't lean over to kiss him goodbye and he didn't seem to notice—or didn't care if he did.

Her feet felt like lead as she trudged toward her house from the driveway. As if with each step she was giving into gravity more and more, becoming heavier and heavier.

Why couldn't she get the sick feeling of impending doom out of her stomach? It was one she recognized, having felt it before and ignored it then. Could she afford to do so now?

But that night, as she lay in her hammock, breathing the eucalyptus-laden air deep into her lungs, wishing she had her necklace to draw strength from, every instinct told her she should worry. The same instinct that she'd ignored prior to her wedding day. Look where that had gotten her... Jilted at the altar.

Why wasn't she picking up her phone and calling Justin? Demanding he tell her what was going on? Better yet, why were tears rolling down her cheeks?

Because she was a fool and she had let him get too close.

She needed to rectify that immediately.

Riley had tossed and turned most of the night, struggled with dragging her butt out of bed that morning to head to work, and then been disappointed that Justin hadn't been on the schedule in the OR.

Disappointed or relieved? Because as long as she didn't see him she didn't have to deal with their changed relationship status.

Why hadn't he called or texted?

Then again, she'd not called or texted him, either.

She could have reached out to him but had instead waited to see what he'd do.

Why?

Because she didn't want to seem desperate to have his attention.

Because he'd made her uncomfortable with his questions about kids.

Because he'd been so distracted by whoever had texted him.

Because she knew he was leaving, and the sooner she accepted it, the sooner she quit wondering, the sooner she could start getting past the heartbreak that was about to rain down on her.

The day crept slowly by, but she made it—never feeling so happy to clock out, go home, shower, and take Daisy for a run.

She ran further than her usual distance, needing to push her body in hopes of clearing her mind. It didn't work, so after returning home she went to her other active therapy—yard work.

She was in the backyard, pulling weeds while Daisy inspected the fence line, when Justin arrived at her house.

"I missed you," he said.

He was there. She was glad he was there. But

he shouldn't be. She needed to *not* get sucked back into those baby blues.

"Daisy, shush," she told the dog, who was yapping at Justin.

Daisy ignored her and kept on barking—wanting Justin to say something to her or to pet her, most likely.

She turned toward this man she was glad to see, but who looking at hurt. Hurt because she felt the tides pulling them apart. And as much as she needed to let go, she desperately wanted to cling.

When Justin stooped to pet Daisy she realized his eyes appeared tired, his face strained—and, despite his words that he'd missed her, he'd stopped just inside the gate rather than come over to her for a welcome kiss.

Did he think she was going to tackle him and lick him crazily, as Daisy was now doing?

"I missed you, too," she admitted, wiping her hands over her shorts and immediately regretting it.

He was clean and crisp in his light blue shirt and khakis, but she was a far cry from it. Other than grabbing a drink, she'd gone straight out to start gardening. She rarely wore gloves while digging around in her flowerbeds, as she preferred the feel of earth against her skin. No doubt dirt streaked her clothes.

"Where were you?" As the question slipped from her mouth she regretted the accusatory tone she heard.

Yes, she'd spent the past twenty-four hours tormenting herself with doubts, but taking that out on him wasn't fair and nor was it what she wanted to do.

"I left the office early and had dinner with my family."

Justin went to his parents every week or so for a meal, usually on the alternate weekend from when he did something with the Wilderness Group. He'd asked her to go several times in the past, but she never had. She usually spent the time catching up on her laundry and housework.

Why had he taken off work early to go today? Had it been a special occasion?

"That's nice. You had a good visit?" She purposely made her tone as pleasant as she could, when her nerve-endings felt as if they'd been scraped with sandpaper.

Justin bent to pet Daisy at last, calming the dog's yapping and eliciting a happy panting. "It was a nice visit."

Ugh. Was she jealous of her dog? It wasn't like she wanted to roll on her back and have him scratch her belly.

Well, no, but…

"My parents are doing well. My sister stopped by with her kids."

He did some more of his looking at Daisy rather than her. Made more small talk.

Looking down at her dirty fingernails, she kept up the awkward trend with a pleasant, "That's good."

"Spending time with family is good." Now his voice was coated with accusation.

She ignored his jab and went on the offensive. "Why didn't you call me?"

"I didn't think you'd want to come," he parried, looking up from where he knelt with Daisy. "You never have in the past."

Riley frowned at his comment, but also at the distance between them. Why was he so far away? Why had he stopped at the gate? Usually he couldn't wait to take her into his arms for a hello kiss when he arrived.

But usually they hadn't disagreed over kids and he hadn't gotten a text message, then shut her out.

"A guy gets tired of hearing no after a while," he added.

Riley flinched. She didn't tell him no often— and never with sex. Just with his attempts to put them into a more traditional relationship box.

Picking up Daisy, he straightened, stroking the dog's fluffy white fur as he said, "Dinner with family usually means a relationship is moving toward certain things. Things that you claim not to want. You've made it clear you don't want them."

Oh, yeah, there was accusation in his tone. Loads of it. And despite his calm petting of Daisy, tension emanated from him.

Riley's knees liquefied, and all she could manage was a muffled, "Oh…"

Moving closer to her, his expression somber, he asked, "That *is* still what you want, Riley?" His narrowed gaze pinned her. "Or, more aptly, *don't* want?"

Feeling a bit woozy, she said, "I— You mean, marriage?"

His eyes not wavering away from hers, he nodded.

What *was* this? Riley wondered. Was Justin telling her he wanted marriage with *her*? Or was this his way of pushing her away?

Which didn't make sense.

He'd come to her house, not the other way around.

But there was something antagonistic about him that she'd never seen before—something dark and stormy, brewing just beneath the surface.

"I… I enjoy our relationship," she admitted. "But I've not changed my mind about marriage."

Just the thought of saying she'd even consider marriage had her stomach twisting. No way did she want to risk feeling again that horrible feeling she'd had when she'd been at her wedding venue alone, when she'd had to tell her guests that Johnny hadn't shown, when she'd had to pretend everything was okay when it hadn't been okay, when *she* hadn't been okay, and then walk away with her head held high even though she'd felt lower than low.

No, she wouldn't be risking that kind of rejection and heartache again.

Taking a step back, Riley inhaled deeply and ordered herself not to let thoughts of Johnny invade a moment when she already felt defensive.

"Where is this coming from?" she asked. "What happened at the museum yesterday? Did your family say something? I feel as if you're wanting to fight with me."

"I don't want to fight—not with you or anyone—and of course my family didn't say anything. They've never met you. Why would they say something?"

His tone said that it was a problem they hadn't met her. Had he wanted her to meet them? He had asked her multiple times in the past, but he'd never acted as if it were a big deal when she said no. The thought of going had practically had her breaking out into hives.

"Why are you so against having children?" he asked.

Eyeing the way he held her dog, stroking Daisy's fur almost methodically, Riley winced. "What relevance does that have to anything? You've known from the beginning how I feel. Why are you making it a big deal now? If you want to break things off, then just do it."

Oh, heavens. Had she really just told Justin to break things off with her? Her heart slapped her for saying such a stupid thing. Logic told her to brace herself for his answer.

Because he'd not come to her house to make things right. He'd come to fight.

But Riley didn't want to fight. She wanted— Justin.

"I'm going to be a dad."

The earth stopped spinning and Riley's body jerked from the force of it.

"What?"

Putting Daisy on the ground, he walked over to the eucalyptus tree and placed his palm against the bark, as if to gain some magical power to continue their conversation.

"I should have said I *hope* to be a dad. If the judge approves my request, I'm adopting Kyle."

"That's wonderful!" she said, and she meant it, joy replacing her anxiety.

Momentarily forgetting their tension, she moved toward him, planning to throw her arms around him, but stopped as she recalled that they were at odds and reality hit.

Justin was adopting Kyle. He'd be a father.

Breathing became difficult… Air was not able to find its way into her contracted lungs. Her knees threatened to wobble, possibly to give out completely and let her drop to the earth, and her mind echoed with one thought.

Justin was going to be a father.

"Not everything is finalized," he continued, his words somehow making their way beyond the noise of her mind, "but after she met with the judge today my lawyer thinks it's going to be. The judge wants proof that I can provide Kyle with a stable life. I spent this afternoon at my parents' putting together an action plan for doing just that."

Justin was adopting Kyle. He was going to be a father. The thoughts continued to race through her mind.

"I want to do what's right for Kyle."

He *would* do what was right for Kyle—would be an excellent father.

"Which is why he's so lucky to have you," she managed to say.

He'd mentioned that Kyle might be up for adoption someday. She'd never considered Justin adopting him—but perhaps she should have, knowing how involved Justin was with him.

She had no doubt Justin would take his position in Kyle's life seriously. The boy was blessed to have Justin wanting to be his father. She didn't find it hard to imagine him being a dad. Justin was wonderful with the boys and would be a wonderful father to Kyle and to any other children he might someday have.

Her uterus spasmed deep within her at the

thought of Justin having more children, of another woman's belly ripe with his baby.

She never should have gotten involved with him. Look at her now, feeling possessive of what wasn't hers, longing for something that hadn't existed for more than a few fleeting moments.

"Riley?"

He interrupted her thoughts and she glanced up, thinking he looked way more perfect than any person had a right to. Definitely he was the closest she'd ever come to perfection—likely ever would come. Not that she was looking for perfection, or anything else. She'd been just fine before he came along. She'd be just fine when he moved on.

Only the thought of not having him in her life gutted her. Not being able to kiss him or touch him.

How was she supposed to forget how it felt to be as one with this man and just move on as if she'd never known that high?

Anger at herself for becoming so vulnerable to him hit her. Anger at herself, and at him too, for making her want things she was better off not wanting.

"Riley?" he repeated.

"Justin?" she countered, lifting her chin and

focusing on her anger. It was easier to grasp hold of than the intense sadness of the fact that they were ebbing away.

Looking frustrated, he raked his fingers though his hair. "I'm trying to figure out where everything in my life stands at this point."

"Mainly meaning me and where I fit in?"

"Kyle adores you."

"I adore him too—but that has nothing to do with where you and I stand."

His gaze bored into her. "Doesn't it?"

A heaviness fell over her chest, her shoulders, weighing her down. Averting her gaze, she stared at her dirty fingernails, wondering why she found feeling the cold earth between her fingers so satisfying, wondering if there was enough dirt on the planet to get her through the heartache headed her way.

"I think we need to talk about Johnny."

Riley's jaw dropped. Um...*no*, they didn't need to do that.

Her fingers curled into her palms. "Why would we talk about my ex?"

"It's time you told me about what happened between the two of you."

It was probably past time. But things had been going along so easily and wonderfully she hadn't wanted to think about Johnny, much less talk about him. Who wanted to tell her lover that the last guy in her bed—the *only* other guy in her bed—had stood her up on what should have been the happiest day of her life?

Telling him now, when they were on the cusp of the end… Did it even matter at this point?

Riley took a deep breath. She didn't want to relive that horrible moment. But Justin wasn't going to let this drop. He thought he needed to know. And maybe telling him would amp up her defenses, because currently she felt so exposed.

"Johnny swooped onto the scene not long after my mother died." She'd felt so alone in the world, so lost…"After she was killed in that car wreck I was devastated." She'd never known a person could cry that many tears and live. "She was my best friend and I'd never felt so alone," she admitted.

She had been alone.

"Johnny was handsome, and charming, and in my grief I latched on to him for all I was worth. Because focusing on him made the pain of losing Mom seem less. I ignored all the things I should have seen—like the fact that he went through half a dozen jobs during the time I knew him—and I dove in heart-first. Because when I was with him I wasn't alone."

"He asked you to marry him."

"Yes, he asked me."

Needing to move, she walked over to the eucalyptus tree, broke off a tiny segment, and inhaled the scent that usually comforted her. Nothing could soothe her inner shaking, though.

"I said yes, and I thought I was the luckiest girl alive when he slipped that engagement ring on my finger."

It hadn't been much of a ring, but she hadn't cared. She'd cherished that thin gold band with a stone that had been a cheap imitation—much as Johnny himself had turned out to be.

"What happened?"

How did she even answer that? Reveal her most humiliating moment? Admit that she hadn't been good enough for Johnny to stay with her so she knew no one ever would. She sure didn't expect someone like Justin to.

"He failed to show up for our wedding."

How could she have been so blind to his true nature? So suckered in by the false compliments that only ever followed his tearing her down first? To his constantly borrowing money? Having her pay for things? She knew the answer, though. Grief had veiled all logic.

She looked at Justin to see how he'd taken her confession.

With a grimace, he narrowed his eyes, and his jaw worked back and forth as he processed what she'd said.

"He was in an accident?"

"That would have been easier in some ways," she admitted. "The truth is more sordid."

She gave a humorless laugh, recalling her utter humiliation when she'd discovered the truth.

"He didn't show up for our wedding because after our rehearsal dinner the night before he'd cashed in our honeymoon airline tickets—" that she had also paid for "—and run off with someone he'd been having an affair with for months."

Wincing, Justin stared at Riley in disbelief that any man could be so stupid. So callous. How did a man just not show up for his own wedding?

"I'm sorry."

Her distaste for marriage was beginning to make sense, as was the determined expression on her face as she stared up at him.

A smudge of dirt across her cheek told the story that she'd brushed her hair back at some point during the past few seconds, prior to putting her hands back on her hips and lifting her chin in defiance at what life had thrown at her.

Her ex really was stupid to have chosen another woman. That the man had hurt her, humiliated her, made her self-conscious about her weight and destroyed her confidence in herself, made Justin want to track him down and beat some sense into him.

Another part wanted to thank him—because had the man been smarter Riley wouldn't be single. And, as frustrated as he was, Justin wouldn't have wanted to have missed out on the past few months.

"Don't be sorry," she advised. "The woman he ran off with did me a favor. Apparently she wasn't the first person he'd cheated on me with, nor would she have been the last."

Her words were said with such fervor that he knew she believed what she said. Good—she *should* believe it. No doubt Johnny hadn't been faithful to the other woman either.

"Once the humiliation and hurt wore off," Riley continued, her chin still tipped upward, "I became grateful he didn't go through with our wedding."

Was that how Ashley had felt? *Grateful*

that he'd called off their wedding because he wouldn't give up his involvement with the boys? At least he'd realized the week before that what they wanted from life didn't mesh, and hadn't left her standing at the altar alone.

But she had felt betrayed, because she hadn't understood how he could put the boys before her. He hadn't been able to explain that he loved them more than he did her, and that giving back to the foster program was something ingrained within him.

"There's something else I need to tell you," he began, wondering how Riley was going to take his next revelation. He didn't want to tell her—knew doing so was going to make her even more prickly—but not to tell her would be wrong.

Not that he was sure it even mattered at this point. Everything in Riley's demeanor said she was already done with him and their relationship. What he was about to tell her would likely destroy any hope that remained.

Not telling her wasn't an option.

"Prior to relocating to Columbia, I was engaged."

If he'd had any doubt as to whether or not she already knew, he no longer did. Her eyes widened, shining with pure shock, and she took a step back, bumping against a tree branch.

"I was nearing the end of my residency, dating a beautiful fellow resident, and knew I wanted a wife and family," he rushed out, knowing he needed to explain. "That's not a good reason for getting engaged, but when she started hinting for a ring I gave her one."

He'd loved kids, wanted a houseful. He'd liked Ashley. They'd gotten along well during their residencies, and he'd believed they could have a good life together. Right up until the moment she'd made that comment about the Wilderness Group and opened his eyes.

"Ashley was a brilliant surgeon…fun. My friends liked her." The more he said, the more Riley's face paled, but he needed to get this out. "We got engaged. Our families were thrilled, as were our friends."

"Please tell me you didn't stand her up."

Riley's voice broke and he'd swear her lower lip trembled.

"No, not exactly. I called off the wedding after I realized I couldn't marry her."

Like Riley, he felt lucky that he'd had a narrow escape from what would have been a miserable marriage for both him and Ashley.

"It sounds as if she was perfect."

Riley's throat worked, and then she surprised him by walking back over to the garden bed where she'd been weeding when he'd arrived and staring down at the plants.

"Why couldn't you marry her?"

"Our definition of 'family' wasn't the same. She wanted me to give up the group…the boys. But they were my family, much more so than she was. I couldn't marry her."

Surely after having spent time with the boys Riley would understand? Despite everything she said she had connected with them, and had formed a special bond with Kyle.

"Honestly, from the moment she called them my 'little charity cases,' anything I felt for her vanished," he admitted, shoving his hands into his pants pockets.

After a few moments Riley dropped to her knees and went back to pulling weeds, as if she hadn't heard him.

Justin stared at her, thinking her reaction odd, waiting for her to say something, to do something other than just pull weeds. He wasn't sure what he'd expected, but not silence, and her going back to what she was doing as if they'd not just had a major heart-to-heart.

"How long before your wedding day did you call things off?"

"The week before we were to be married."

Her hands stilled. "At least you didn't leave her at the venue, waiting for you to arrive."

The extent to which Johnny had betrayed her hit home. The man truly had let her go to the last minute before letting her realize what a loser he was.

Had he not realized until right before the wedding that Ashley only tolerated the Wilderness Group, and planned for him to give it up after they married, would he have gone through with *his* wedding?

"I wouldn't do that," he assured her, even as he simultaneously acknowledged to himself that he couldn't say the same about Ashley.

Her hands squeezed the dirt. "Of that I have no doubt."

There was an ominous overtone to her words. "Meaning?"

Letting go of the dirt, she let it sift out through her fingers. "I'd never give you the opportunity to dump me at the altar."

"I *didn't* dump Ashley at the altar." Maybe he almost had, but he'd had a good reason. "She was fine." Not at first, but she had moved on.

"She's planning a big wedding with her new fiancé."

Ashley had moved on, and from the outside looking in she seemed no worse for wear. But was that what Johnny thought about Riley?

Riley grabbed hold of a weed and yanked hard. "You keep tabs on her?"

"No, but we dated for a long time."

They'd been so busy with med school, then residency, that neither had realized they wanted different things. If only they'd spent more time talking they'd have saved a lot of heartache.

"She and my mother have stayed in touch."

That sounded chummier than it was. The reality was that they ran into each other at various events and chatted. Other than a rare phone conversation or birthday card, neither sought out the other as far as he knew.

"Your mother told you about your ex's wedding plans at your visit today?"

Riley yanked at the stubborn weed again, almost falling back when she lost her grip. Had he been closer, he'd have tried to steady her, but he was too far away so he just nodded. He realized Riley wasn't looking his way, and said, "Yes."

After he'd told his mother about his plans to adopt Kyle, she'd launched into tales of Ashley.

"You didn't find that odd? Does she want you to intervene and win her back?"

"No."

At least, he hadn't gotten the impression that had been his mother's goal. Nor had he found her comment odd—more reflective on how life changed.

"She was just musing about how Ashley was planning another wedding and I was planning to adopt, how we were both happy, and how things changed with time. She wasn't hinting that we should get back together."

"It's good to have someone to support you unconditionally."

Yes, it was. It was what he'd hoped to find someday—what he'd hoped to have with Riley.

"I'm blessed with a great family." Which was probably why it was so important to him to have a big family of his own. "Just as Stephen has been."

Riley's hands stilled.

"Things could have been so different," he continued, thinking back over what he could recall of his early childhood. "When I was placed with Mom and Dad they adopted me. I hope to do the same for Kyle—to give him what I've had."

And he wanted Riley to be a part of that. Even

with the turmoil of emotions whipping through him, that remained clear. He wanted Riley in his life.

Moving to stand near her, he held out his hand to help her back to her feet. "I'd like you to be a part of my life—a part of Kyle's life."

She didn't look up from where she still tugged on the persistent weed, and nor did she take his outstretched hand. Her shoulders drooped a little.

Letting go of the weed, she held up her hand—not to take his, but to make a "stop" motion. "Don't say anything more. I let myself get caught up in a relationship with you when I knew better. That was a mistake. A big one. But that doesn't mean I have to keep making it."

Heart racing, Justin stared down at where she knelt on the ground. He was opening himself up to her, laying everything on the line and telling her he wanted her in his life.

She was calling them a mistake.

It wouldn't surprise him if she buried herself in the ground in an effort to block him out.

"Riley, I don't think you understand what I'm trying to say," he began, thinking if he could only make her understand she'd quit shutting him out.

"You're the one who doesn't understand. How could you? You've never felt the things I've felt…never been humiliated by the person you trusted most." She took a deep breath. "I'd like you to leave."

"Riley…" he began, knowing that leaving would be an even bigger mistake than either of them had made already. "Stand up and look at me. We need to talk this through. My leaving won't solve anything."

Surely she had to see that? Had to see that he wanted her in his life. In Kyle's life.

"Your leaving will solve *everything.*"

Because she wanted to shield herself rather than face what was happening between them, rather than let him in.

"I want you to go," she continued.

He reached out to touch her, but she jerked away.

"Don't touch me."

Justin's hand fell. Riley was so far gone emotionally he'd never get through to her until she'd had time to think, to realize they were worth taking a chance on.

"I'll call later—once you've had time to calm down."

"I won't change my mind."

"About?"

"Us."

That was when it fully sank in. Riley was done. This wasn't just a disagreement. To Riley, this was the end. She'd just thrown away their relationship.

How could she do that? Be willing to do that? As if they didn't have something special? As if he didn't matter?

Perhaps for the first time he understood how Ashley had felt when she'd asked him those same questions. His answer had been easy at the time. He hadn't loved her.

Just as Riley didn't love him.

Although she'd yet to get that persistent deeply rooted weed, she began pulling stray bits of grass from the garden bed—as if nothing significant was happening, as if she'd grown bored with the conversation.

As if she wasn't tearing them apart.

Justin stared down at her, gutted, letting a myriad of emotions filter through him and settling on a mix of resignation and anger.

Why was he doing this? She didn't want what he wanted, didn't have the same feelings he did. He just needed to accept it.

"Fine—there is no us." Each word felt like

a razor, scraping his insides before it left his mouth. "I guess there never really was. You have your life and I have mine."

He turned, quietly let himself out through her gate, making sure Daisy was safely on the other side, and walked away.

Like she'd said—problem solved.

CHAPTER ELEVEN

"Where are Riley and Daisy?" Kyle asked, as the boy realized Riley and the dog weren't waiting for them in the Jeep.

Justin had been dreading Kyle's question, but had known the boy would ask. Of course the kid would.

Riley hadn't missed a single excursion for the past three months, and if it was something the dog could go to neither had Daisy.

Kyle and Daisy had formed a special bond.

As had he and Riley.

The fact that she wasn't in the front passenger seat said everything, driving home what had been Justin's reality this past week and a half.

It's what she wants, he reminded himself.

What he wanted, too—because he was tired of chasing a woman who didn't want to be chased.

Justin checked Kyle's seatbelt, making sure the boy had gotten it secured properly. "Riley won't be here today."

Kyle's sandy brows rose and he stared at Justin from where he sat in the passenger side back seat. "Why not?"

Good question, and one Justin struggled with answering. Because he didn't understand exactly how they'd gone from talking to her telling him to leave. How had their conversation ended with them ending? He'd come to bare his soul to her and instead he'd walked away.

Maybe he shouldn't have left.

But he hadn't been able to stay when she was telling him to leave. Telling him not to touch her.

Oh, how that had hurt. That she hadn't been able to bear his touch. That she'd rather be alone than with him.

His muscles seized his ribcage, crushing inward. He put his hand on the roll bar, leaned in a little. "Riley's busy."

Probably working in her yard, running, or out doing something with Cassie. She and Sam were off again, so the two women had lots of time to console each other.

"Too busy for us?" Kyle didn't look as if he believed Justin.

"She has things to do, bud, besides just hang out with a bunch of guys."

The boy's forehead scrunched deeper. "Doesn't she like us anymore? I can tell her sorry if I did something wrong."

That the boy immediately thought it was something *he'd* done wrong broke Justin's heart. Especially since it wasn't Kyle who had messed up. Justin hadn't messed up either. Other than to want more than Riley did.

"You didn't do anything wrong," he assured him.

Getting Kyle beyond that, to where he didn't immediately question himself, and giving the boy the confidence to know he was worthy and wanted was something Justin would spend the rest of his life making sure happened.

Kyle considered him a moment. "Did *you* do something wrong?"

Justin laughed at the boy's perceptiveness. "Probably," he admitted.

After all, hadn't Riley accused him of wanting to fight moments after he'd arrived at her place? Had he gone there looking to fight with her? Knowing which buttons to push to get a rise out of her?

But why? Why would he do that? He hadn't wanted to fight with her. He'd had everything to lose and nothing to gain.

In some ways he *had* lost everything.

At the hospital, Riley had transferred out of the operating room to work on the orthopedic floor. With Cassie still out with her knee, she'd been able to easily make the transition, and thus far had managed to avoid providing care for any of his patients.

She'd probably asked not to have any of his patients.

She'd neatly shut him out of her life.

He'd been a fool to think something special was happening between them, that she was different…

Justin tapped the roll bar with the side of his fisted hand. He gave one last look at Kyle's safety belt, secured around his booster seat, then climbed into the driver's seat.

He'd not even gotten his seatbelt fastened when Kyle asked, "Did you tell her you were sorry?"

Sorry for what? Caring about her? Wanting her in his life?

Justin's gaze cut to Kyle's via the rearview mirror. "Unfortunately there's some things 'sorry' can't fix."

Kyle gave him an empathetic look. "My teacher at school says it's always a good place to start."

"Smart teacher." Justin started the Jeep and tuned the radio to a station he knew Kyle liked.

When they arrived at the bowling alley Stan was already there with the other kids. Including Kyle and Stephen, there were six boys. Maybe a few stragglers would still show.

Justin hoped so, as he always worried about the kids who didn't make it for their activities.

They'd reserved two lanes, so divided themselves into two groups to bowl. Stan took one team of three boys and Justin took the other.

The afternoon passed quickly enough, and soon they were eating pizza. The boys finished their meal, picked up their trash, then ran back to start another game while Justin and Stan divvied up what was left of the pizza to send home with the kids.

"You driving Kyle home?" Stan asked.

Stacking the boxes, Justin nodded. "I've made arrangements with his foster parents to spend some extra time with him. He seemed excited that I was picking him up."

"No wonder. He idolizes you." Stan grinned. "Have you told him yet?"

Justin shook his head. "I didn't think it would be fair to tell him before all the papers were signed, just in case something changes between now and then. If all goes well, he'll be mine next Monday."

Stan nodded as if he understood. And as the man had adopted Stephen, perhaps he did.

"I kept worrying that something would go wrong, that no one was just going to give me a kid as great as Stephen to love forever. I didn't even realize I was holding my breath until I could tuck him in that first night, knowing he was mine and we were his."

Yeah, that pretty much summed up how Justin felt. Like he was holding his breath.

He'd managed to turn his spare room into a decent boy's bedroom. Soon he and Kyle could go house-hunting and the kid could help him pick out their new home. Justin already had an agent looking, but so far nothing had appealed.

Because nothing had a magical back yard.

Ugh.

He had to get past everything to do with Riley.

"What's up with you and Riley?"

Turning toward his friend, Justin grimaced. "Not you, too?"

Stan laughed. "Kyle grilling you?"

Justin nodded and took a sip of his water.

"That kid is crazy about her and Daisy."

There was that…

Stan gave him a brotherly slap on the arm. "Maybe you should just marry her and keep her around permanently."

Justin choked on the drink he'd just taken and coughed to clear his throat. "That's *not* happening."

Stan looked disappointed. "Too bad. I thought you made a good couple. Is that why she's not here?"

"You have it wrong. She's the one who won't commit. Not me."

Not him. He wanted a committed relationship with Riley. *Had* wanted. Because he was past that now. Now he just wanted to give Kyle a wonderful life. Not to be with someone who shut him out with their first fight.

Wrong. She'd shut him out from the beginning. He'd just been too foolish to accept it.

Stan appeared shocked. "I've seen how she looks at you. She's in love with you. I'd bet money on it."

Justin's chest tightened at his friend's observation. "You've got that wrong, too, pal. That was lust in her eyes, not love."

"Maybe…but she sure fooled me." Stan looped his thumbs into his pockets. "I take it you're not together anymore?"

Justin shook his head.

"Sorry to hear that."

"It was inevitable." Riley had never wanted anything long-term.

"Again, I'm surprised. You two were much better suited than you and Ashley ever were. You never meshed."

Justin frowned at his friend. This was the first time Stan had ever commented on Ashley. "Seriously? Everyone always told me how shocked they were that we broke up."

Stan looked surprised. "I wasn't shocked you broke things off—just at how long you took to do so. On the few times she came to one of the Wilderness Group get-togethers you never looked at her the way you looked at Riley. Not once."

Probably not. Because he'd never felt about Ashley the way he felt about Riley. Which meant what?

Nothing. Because she'd never let her guard down long enough to risk love and he'd forever be walking on eggshells in case she shut him out.

She *had* shut him out.

"Call it lust or love or whatever, but you were

never heartbroken over your break-up with Ashley—unlike now."

Justin shook his head in denial. "You're just seeing nerves. Once everything is settled and Kyle is officially mine I'll be fine."

"If you say so." Stan's gaze went to where the kids were cheering as Jevon's ball knocked down half the pins. "Let's go see what the boys are up to."

Justin walked into the spare bedroom, his gaze going to the stuffed video character on the bed. Kyle's favorite. Justin had covered the bed with a matching comforter set, and hung a few posters on the wall, but the room was still bare basics because he wanted Kyle involved in the process of decorating. He'd just got a few items to make the kid feel welcome.

If he got to bring him home.

Maybe he just *thought* he was meant to have a houseful of kids.

Maybe his role was simply to run the Wilderness Group and he shouldn't try to take things further.

He'd always planned to adopt. But was it fair of him to project that onto the people in his life? To have projected it upon Ashley? Upon Riley?

Just the thought of her had his insides knotted.

He'd wanted forever. She'd wanted—not forever.

Not anything.

Raking his fingers through his hair, he went back to his own room and got ready for bed.

When he climbed between the sheets he was still restless. Because he couldn't get Riley off his mind. Knowing sleep wasn't going to happen, he grabbed his phone off the nightstand and opened his messages.

Nothing.

Not one word from her.

What was he thinking? She wasn't going to text him. If she'd wanted to talk to him she wouldn't have done everything she could to put space between them. So why couldn't he just forget her?

He tapped her number, pulling up her text messages and scrolling back to when she'd sent him the photos of them during that first run.

His jaw worked back and forth as memories assaulted him. Memories of how vulnerable she'd been—still was, he reminded himself. Memories of how kissing her that first time had felt, in the garden at Paul and Cheyenne's engagement party. Memories of their first night together in the very bed he now lay in.

No wonder his house felt empty.

No wonder every house the real estate agent had shown him had felt empty.

Because *he* was empty.

Empty without Riley.

He'd been a fool to hope he could change her mind. Change her heart.

Memories of the past flashed through him—memories of hoping he could change his birth mother's heart, could make her want him. He couldn't make Riley love him any more than he'd been able to make his birth mother love him.

He consoled himself that just as he'd made a new life with the Brothers family—a much better life than he'd had—he'd now do the same with Kyle.

Sighing, he went to put his phone on the nightstand and missed. His phone clanged down between the bed and the piece of furniture.

Sitting up in bed, he flipped on the lamp, and looked in the space between his bed and the nightstand, expecting to see his phone.

He didn't. It must have landed beneath the bed.

Getting up, he knelt on the floor and felt

around for his phone, but still didn't see it in the shadows.

"Great," he muttered, opening the nightstand's top drawer and pulling out a flashlight.

Bending down, he shone the light into the shadows, spotting his phone where it had landed.

A golden glint reflected in the flashlight's beam was what he reached for, though. And his hand shook as he closed his fingers around the gold chain with its tiny cross.

He'd found Riley's necklace.

"Men are stupid," Cassie murmured, tossing a flower petal onto the ground.

As her friend stretched out on the bench Riley sat across from her in a chair, opposite the burned low fire in the pit. Daisy lazed in her lap, only opening her eyes long enough to look up and nudge Riley's hand when it stilled in stroking her back.

"Agreed."

"I mean, Sam should have called by now."

Which meant her friend was waiting for him to call. Riley fought against wincing. Would Cassie never learn? She and Sam had been doing this on-again, off-again for years.

"Don't you think it's time to call it quits for good with Sam?" she asked.

Cassie gave her an *Are you crazy?* look. "Why would I think that? I love him."

Riley frowned. "Then why aren't you with him?"

Cassie gave her a point-blank stare. "Why aren't you with Justin?"

Justin. She didn't want to talk about him. Or think about him. Doing either hurt too much.

"The two have nothing to do with each other," she assured.

Cassie had the audacity to snort. "Yeah, right. You've sniffed this eucalyptus one time too many."

"It's not the same," she defended, but even to her own ears her words sounded weak. Which didn't make sense. She didn't love Justin. "I do miss him," she admitted.

Of course she missed him. She'd had a great time with him.

And not just the sex. It was more the way he made her laugh, made her see the world in vivid colors, made her feel young and silly—beautiful, even. He'd made her step outside her comfort zone.

Ha. That wasn't what she missed. That was

what had been their downfall. Him trying to push her beyond her comfort zone.

"Do you miss him with all your being? To the point that you'd do just about anything to hear him say your name? To see his smile? Hear his laughter? Feel his touch?" Cassie continued, her voice becoming more and more emotional as she did so. "'Cause that's the way I miss Sam."

Her roommate's words dinged at her like pointed darts, hitting their target. Riley did miss Justin in all those ways.

"If Sam hasn't called by tomorrow I'm calling him," Cassie announced.

Riley felt sorry for her friend. "Oh, Cassie, are you sure?"

"Absolutely. He's mine."

Cassie's certainty stunned Riley. "How do you know? I mean, you're not together..."

"We've had a fight." Cassie shrugged. "I don't like it, but it's what we do. Just like we make up. We do that really well, too."

Riley shook her head. "Aren't you afraid that someday you won't make up? That eventually he's going to walk away and not come back?"

Cassie gave her that look again. "Why would I be afraid of that?"

"Why *wouldn't* you?"

"Because he loves me," Cassie said, with so much confidence Riley couldn't question the sentiment. "Just as I love him. A disagreement—a thousand disagreements—won't ever change that. We'll always make up."

Riley stared. "I… I guess I understand that."

"If you feel about Justin the way I think you do, then you do understand. When you love someone you can't not make up because you can't imagine life without them."

Looking beyond her friend to her fairy tree, she saw the place where she'd rebuilt her life, established a home and found peace. Had she really made an oasis away from reality? Or a fort to hide within?

Nothing wrong with a home being an oasis or a place where one felt protected, she assured herself.

"You should call him," Cassie suggested. "As in right now—pick up your phone and call him."

Riley rolled her eyes. "What exactly is it you'd have me say if I did?"

"The truth. That you miss him and are sorry for whatever happened between the two of you."

"I didn't do anything wrong," she defended, although she wasn't sure she was telling the truth.

"You didn't do anything right or he'd still be here."

"Well, if that isn't the pot calling the kettle black!" she shot at her friend.

"You're right. I'm calling Sam." Cassie pulled her cell from her pocket and punched in Sam's number. Scooting into a sitting position, she got up, then hobbled toward the house. When she reached the back door, she gave Riley a pointed look, then said into the phone, "Hey, baby, I miss you…"

No doubt her friend would make up with Sam and they'd act as if nothing happened. Until the next time.

"That's not the life for me," she said aloud, causing Daisy to lift her head in question. "Who needs all that drama?"

Not that her relationship with Justin had been filled with drama. It hadn't.

She thought Cassie was crazy, but she envied her friend that faith in Sam. What would it feel like to be that loved?

Exactly the way Justin loved you before you pushed him away.

Oh, how Riley hated that nagging voice in her head.

Justin hadn't loved her. He'd—

Why had he even spent the last few months with her? There had to be easier relationships for him than one with a girl who was jaded about love and had been jilted at the altar, like her.

Yet he'd stuck by her, showered her with affection despite her struggling to give him any back outside of their physical relationship.

Why?

He could so easily have been done with her after she'd left that first night. Instead he'd reached out to her, nurtured their relationship, tried to make her feel safe.

But she'd been as prickly as a briar bush for fear of getting hurt. And ultimately she'd pushed him away. And hurt him. Hurt herself, too.

She closed her eyes. What had she done?

She needed to tell Justin that she missed him so much she felt as if she'd lost a part of herself. Not going out with him and the boys today had hurt so much.

Cassie's description ran through her mind. She did feel that way about Justin. All those ways. She couldn't imagine going through life without ever seeing him smile at her again, without hearing her name on his lips, without placing her hand over his heart and feeling the strong beat there. The beat that was for her.

Because Justin cared about her.

At least he *had*.

She had to go to him. She didn't know what would happen, but she'd tell him she missed him, that she was sorry she'd shut him out for fear of getting hurt. Tell him that being without him hurt. She didn't have a plan beyond that, but at least it was a start.

She'd only taken a few steps when she stopped.

Sitting in her driveway was Justin's Jeep.

CHAPTER TWELVE

FOR THE MILLIONTH time Justin asked himself what he was doing in Riley's driveway.

He hadn't had to bring the necklace to her tonight. He could have just given it to her at work the following day. So why had he gotten dressed and driven straight to her house? Better yet, why had he been sitting in her driveway for the past five minutes?

There was enough glow coming from behind the house that he knew he'd find Riley out back. Was she lying on the hammock where they'd made love? Or was she perched beneath the fairy tree she loved so much?

Bark. Bark. Bark.

Justin glanced through the windshield, made out Riley's outline in the dim light. Riley was there, holding Daisy, but bent to let the dog free. Daisy immediately took off toward him, yapping frantically and jumping up into the Jeep.

"Hey, girl," he greeted her when Daisy leapt

up into his lap and began licking his face. Despite his tension, Justin laughed. "Yeah, I missed you, too."

He loved on the dog for a second, then took a deep breath as he glanced back toward where Riley had been standing.

She was gone.

Great. Had she gone into the house, or around back again? He'd wondered if she'd let him in, or if she'd take the necklace and then tell him to leave again. He had Daisy. She'd have to talk to him long enough to get her dog back, to hear him out as he told her what was in his heart.

"Okay, girl, let's go talk to your mom and hope she's as happy to see me as you are," he said, before moving her from his lap to the passenger seat. "What are the odds she'll greet me like you did? Jumping in my lap and licking my face would be one heck of an icebreaker."

"Is that what you want?"

Shocked at the unexpected question, Justin glanced up. Riley stood near the driver's side.

"Me to jump in your lap and lick your face?"

Stunned that she'd heard his comment, that he'd not known she was there and had said something so stupid, he scowled at Daisy. "Don't you know you're supposed to give me notice when someone walks up to the car?"

"Apparently she was too busy licking you to notice."

"Apparently," he agreed, taking in everything about Riley.

She wore a loose T-shirt and yoga pants. Her hair was up in a ponytail and not a speck of makeup covered her face.

"You're beautiful," he said.

Not exactly what he'd meant to say, but true.

"Thanks, but I'm still not doing a Daisy impersonation by jumping in your lap and licking your face."

Justin stared at her, not quite able to believe that she was teasing him. Or that she hadn't told him to leave. It was what he'd been expecting.

Maybe—just maybe—she'd listen to what he had to say. If he could find the right words, that was. He sure hadn't during the time he'd been sitting in her driveway, wondering what he was going to say now that he was here.

"But I will hop in for a ride, if you're okay with that?" She looked at him in question, waiting for his response.

Justin swallowed. Maybe he hadn't really gotten out of bed and found her necklace. Maybe instead he'd just drifted off to sleep and was dreaming.

"Hop in."

She started to climb in, then paused. "I'm going to put Daisy inside." She looked uncertain. "Will you wait for me?"

Forever.

Forever?

Grateful he hadn't said the word out loud, for fear she wouldn't come back outside, he nodded.

She scooped up the dog, talked to her the whole way to the house, then let her into the screened-in side porch, closing the door and making sure the latch caught.

What was she saying to the dog? Probably warning her to send out a search party if she hadn't returned within a reasonable amount of time.

He leaned back against the headrest, stared up at the sky, and tapped his fingers against the steering wheel.

Forever. That was what had echoed through him when she'd asked him if he'd wait. But she didn't want the same things he did. Not just that, but she specifically *didn't* want the things he dreamed of.

Would she ever?

If not, how far was he willing to go to keep her in his life?

How much was he willing to give up?

"You okay?" she asked, climbing in beside him and fastening her seatbelt.

"Not really," he admitted, knowing he hadn't been okay since their disagreement at the children's museum. "Where do you want to go?"

"Anywhere. Just drive."

Justin started the engine and took off down her street. The wind noise made talking impossible unless they wanted to yell at each other.

He drove them down toward the river, through several sections of town, and kept driving until he realized he'd circled back to near her house.

Rather than go into her driveway, he pulled into the neighborhood park and killed the engine near the bandshell.

They'd walked down here and sat in one of the carved-out seats in the natural amphitheater built into the hillside and listened to bands on more than one occasion. Tonight the only light shining was the moon, but it lit the path down the hill.

"Walk with me?" he asked.

She hesitated only a second, then nodded.

He met her on her side of the Jeep, and then,

knowing he might be slapped down, took her hand into his.

She didn't pull away.

Her hand felt small in his—small, warm, soft, and yet capable.

She'd been hurt so badly. He couldn't imagine how she'd felt being stood up at her own wedding. No wonder she refused to give anyone the opportunity to hurt her again.

They walked down to the empty bandshell, and before he could suggest it Riley sat on the edge of the stage. Without letting go of his hand. Instead, she held on tight, as if she was afraid of letting go.

"I've missed you."

Her softly spoken words were the sweetest music that had ever played on that stage.

Humbled by her admission, he lifted her hand to his lips and pressed a kiss there. "Not nearly as much as I've missed you."

"I'm sorry."

Her words sliced into him, ripping his insides to shreds. He remembered how he'd balked at her self-preservation on the day Mary had texted him. Shame filled him.

"I'm the one who's sorry. You were right. I

came looking to fight that night. I didn't real-ize—not even after you pointed it out."

Her hand shook in his. "It doesn't matter."

"It does," he corrected, knowing that he couldn't stop until he'd told her what was in his heart. "It mattered enough that it drove a wedge between us."

"Because I let it." She took a deep breath. "No, I did more than let it. I drove it as deep as I could."

"Because I scared you?"

Her lower lip trembled, as if corroborating her next statement. "I'm terrified of you."

"I don't want you to be scared, Riley. That's not how I want you to feel about me."

He stepped close, wrapped his arms around her. She didn't pull away. Instead she leaned into his arms, resting against him. *Forever*, he thought again. That was how long he'd wait for her. How long he'd fight for her. How long he'd be hers.

"I don't want to be afraid anymore."

His heart knotted at her sweet admission. "Tell me how I can help," he said. "What I can do to make things right. I'll do whatever it takes."

Looking down at her hand in his, she gave a little squeeze, and said, "Then love me."

* * *

Riley couldn't believe she'd made the plea. That she'd let Justin guess at how vulnerable she was.

Guess? *Ha.* She'd pretty much spelled it out for him.

"That's all?" He laced his fingers with hers. "I thought you were going to ask me to do something difficult, like slay dragons or thwart evil masterminds."

"No evil masterminds or dragons. It's just my own insecurities imprisoning me."

"Then let me free you." He squeezed her hand, looked into her eyes. "I love you, Riley."

Riley's heart leapt at his words. His very unexpected words. Johnny had tossed the phrase at her so freely, never meaning them. Justin had never spoken the words to her before. Not once. Until now.

Wanting to believe him, but unable to foil her fears, she pressed her forehead to his. "You're sure?"

"You doubt me?"

Her hands shook and she held on to his tighter. "No, Justin. I don't doubt you."

She'd doubted herself—doubted that she could handle losing someone so precious. She almost had.

"You have no reason to doubt me, Riley. I'm yours."

Hers? Was it even possible?

"For however long you'll have me." He swallowed. "Longer than that. Whether you'll risk loving me, risk letting me be a part of your life or not, you are a part of mine and always will be. Because my heart is yours."

Riley's eyes stung. Tears trickled down her face as she admitted, "I love you, Justin. Kyle, too. But I—what if I can't do this? What if I lock up every time we start getting closer and push you away?"

He kissed her hands, held them tightly within his. "Then I'll love you through it."

Was it even possible?

"I used to want children, a family, but then…"

"But then you got left at the altar and decided being alone was safer than risking that devastation again?"

Her insides quivered at what he was saying, at how exposed she was making her heart.

Then again, her heart was more than exposed. Her heart was Justin's.

"I can't believe I haven't told you why I was in your driveway," he said suddenly.

Confused, she watched him reach into his

pocket and pull out a gold chain. Realizing what he held, disbelief hit her. Her breath caught all over again.

"My necklace!"

"I found it earlier tonight. It's been beneath my bed." He took her hand, pressed the necklace into her palm and closed her fingers around the chain. "The clasp is broken, but I'll have it repaired."

The chain had been in his pocket, and the metal was warm against her skin. Or maybe it was the warmth emanating from within her because he'd found her precious gift.

Oh, Mama, she thought, squeezing the chain. *How I wish that you were here...that you could know Justin.*

"I can't believe you found it after all this time. I thought I'd lost it forever." Her eyes watered as she looked up at him. "Even worse, I thought I'd lost *you* forever."

His eyes glittered with the reflection of the moon. *"You* are my forever, Riley."

Justin kissed her—a kiss not quite like any they'd shared. A kiss that was full of the ever-present heat, but also full of possessiveness and giving. *Love,* she thought. *That's what is there.*

It had been there all along, but she'd been too defensive to accept it.

Never again. Come what may, she'd lay her heart at his feet, risking him trampling it or lifting it high. She'd take his precious heart and cherish the gift of his love.

EPILOGUE

"He'll be here," Cassie assured Riley, rearranging her veil.

Understanding why her friend felt the need to reassure her, yet again, Riley resisted being annoyed at her friend's repeated comment. Her friend's unnecessary comment.

Justin *would* be here.

As long as there was breath in his body he'd be there for her and for Kyle and for any other children who came along.

Still, she did currently question her sanity at not insisting they just go to the county clerk's office and say their vows there.

"You ready?" asked Cassie.

"Ready for this to be over."

Riley looked in the mirror one last time. She'd not lost that fifteen pounds she'd meant to lose before today, but it didn't matter. What mattered was how Justin's eyes lit up when he looked at her…how when he looked at her what he saw was everything he wanted.

Cassie scowled at her answer. "This is the best day of your life. Enjoy it."

Riley laughed. "Which means tonight is going to be the best night of my life, right? That I *will* enjoy."

Catching on, Cassie widened her eyes, then giggled. "*Now* I understand your rush. Let's get this show on the road."

"Thank you," she told her friend. "For being here with me today, and the last time I planned to do this, too."

"I wouldn't be anywhere else." Cassie leaned in for a quick hug, taking care with Riley's dress and makeup. "Who would have thought you'd be married before me?"

"Just by a few weeks," Riley reminded her.

Cassie held up her left hand, flashing her diamond solitaire. "At which time you get to return the favor and walk down the aisle with me."

But Riley wasn't walking down an aisle, *per se*. Just taking a car down to the bandshell, where their friends, all the Wilderness Group, and Justin's family were waiting.

And Justin.

He'd be there.

Cassie helped Riley into her car. It wasn't a long walk, but far enough that she wasn't making the trek in a wedding gown.

A parking spot had been reserved for her near the top of the amphitheater, just out of view of the stage.

"About time you showed up," Sam said as he helped Riley out of the car. "Your groom is nervous you're not going to show."

Riley shook her head. "He knows better. The only place I'm going is wherever he is."

Simple traditional bridal music began playing. Sam leaned over, kissed Cassie, then kissed Riley's cheek before going to take his seat.

Cassie hugged Riley one last time, then moved forward to where she would make her way to Justin. Riley couldn't see the stage, so she waited until the music changed before moving forward.

She moved to the top of the hillside, where she looked down at her guests, all of whom had stood at the change in music and turned to face her.

A flashback of stepping out at her previous wedding hit her—that moment when she'd appeared in order to tell everyone that the groom had bailed and there would be no wedding.

But the rising panic died as quickly as it had come to life as her gaze settled on the wonderful man standing on the stage waiting for her, with a sandy-haired imp standing next to him in a matching suit.

Mine, she thought as she made her way to her soon-to-be husband, who was smiling back at her with his heart in his eyes.

Her heart. Her family. Today and forever.

And it was.

* * * * *

LET'S TALK
Romance

For exclusive extracts, competitions
and special offers, find us online:

- 📘 facebook.com/millsandboon
- 📷 @millsandboonuk
- 🐦 @millsandboon

Or get in touch on 0844 844 1351*

For all the latest titles coming soon,
visit millsandboon.co.uk/nextmonth

Want even more
ROMANCE?

Join our bookclub today!

'Mills & Boon books, the perfect way to escape for an hour or so.'

Miss W. Dyer

'Excellent service, promptly delivered and very good subscription choices.'

Miss A. Pearson

'You get fantastic special offers and the chance to get books before they hit the shops'

Mrs V. Hall

Visit millsandbook.co.uk/Bookclub and save on brand new books.

MILLS & BOON